I0630872

## Praise for *Suburban Death Project*

The Gothic tales that constitute Aimee Parkison's *Suburban Death Project* tend to occur in rural settings with woods and water, which contribute to the nightmarish afflictions that torment her characters. The afflictions' unexpectedness, along with the subject matter and deceptive *sangfroid* of the prose, resemble that master of the uncanny, Patricia Highsmith. High praise.

**Harold Jaffe,** Fulbright and NEA Fellow, and author of 28 books

In Aimee Parkison's *Suburban Death Project,* mysteries abound: insect actors, the DNA of extinct animals preserved in tattoos, a dildo in lapis lazuli, and, above it all, the mystery of just what brave new world of storytelling is this? Playful and effortlessly pleasurable, Parkison's *Project* is also powerfully human.

**Curtis White,** Essayist, experimental fiction writer, and author of 15 books

Who owns the body? Who owns the self? Who can measure the unfathomable future and can we trust them to tell their findings true? In Parkison's superb new collection, women escape their childhoods by succumbing to their magic; or mourn their husbands by tasting the fruit that grows from their bodies; or claim their destiny by abandoning it to the world. These are stories of blood — almost written in it — but they are rarely stories of violence even when violent acts occur. Rather, Parkison's wives and daughters, ghosts and surgeons, widows, witnesses, lovers of the night and the deep, dark waters imbue these tales with blood that pulses even as it spills. These are terrible tales that echo like prophecy as they underline, again and again, the inescapably beautiful now. Reader, beware, here the map ends.

**Sarah Blackman,** Author of *of Mother Box* and *Hex*

Parkison is a master of the densely coiled secrets that run rampant within the body/couple/suburb/structure. Nothing is left unmined through this explosive collection packed with subterfuge of gaslighting, stalking and what keeps the game of predator/prey interesting and provocative. *Suburban Death Project* scrapes the nerves and pierces the heart. Parkison detonates and mesmerizes.

**Meg Tuite**, Author of *Meet My Haze*


Stephen Dunn once argued that "the good poem maintains a delicate balance between strangeness and familiarity," that it "must make the familiar strange enough to be re-seen or re-felt by the reader." In that sense — as well as in the lyricism of her exacting sentences — the stories in *Suburban Death Project* are poems. These stories — inhabited by such figures as an amputee who fishes for owls, a woman who can't stop laughing after her husband's suicide and who ends up eating his sadness in a peach, and the legend of a runaway girl who lives in a lighthouse and haunts the tunnels of a seaside cave — will startle the reader, it's true, in the manner that Robert Frost was speaking of when he posited his famous dictum, "No tears in the writer, no tears in the reader. No surprise for the writer, no surprise for the reader." These compelling and memorable fictions will surprise you, and, yes, disturb you, but they will also move you, and reawaken you to the strangeness of the familiar world, and in so doing they will allow you to return to it as if for the first time, as if it were once again a garden.

**George Looney**, Author of *The Worst May Be Over* and *Ode to the Earth in Translation*

# Previous Praise for Aimee Parkison

Parkison makes absurd that which is commonplace by twisting it into abnormality. Lyrical and often abstract, these seemingly linked stories call attention to the grotesque in modern society. ... One is moved equally by the lyricism and repulsiveness and can find beauty in both. A poetic and purposefully perverse collection of stories that describes a dystopian world only slightly divergent from our own.

*Kirkus Reviews*

Like so many of her generation, raised entirely within the reach of visual technology, Aimee Parkison, whose stories have garnered both critical praise and prestigious awards, maintains a voyeur's densely layered dynamic with the world. In these newest stories, it is easy to get seduced as much by the sonic texture of her accomplished prose as by its startling cinematic imagery. But make no mistake — Parkison is a storyteller, conjuring characters who harbor festering secrets, lurid urgencies, and violent compulsions. Like Joyce Carol Oates, Parkison deftly works the caricatures of Southern Gothicism into terrifying clarity.

*Review of Contemporary Fiction*

As a writer, Aimee Parkison is what my younger female colleagues admiringly call a badass bitch. Winner of the FC2 Catherine Doctorow Innovative Fiction Prize, these linked comic-horror stories carry you off into an alternate dark gleaming world that is spookily akin to our own. Overtly poetic, Parkison's language delivers the strangest of songs — she enjoys lulling the reader in a sort of chilly romantic doze so as to wake her up into a world where poor women sell their faces (only to mourn the loss forever) and rich women wear babies' eyes as jewelry. Daring and unforgettable.

*TANK Magazine*

Aimee Parkison most often begins softly, slowly stripping away each layer of social interaction to get at what is numinous and frightening and necessary about living in the real world. These are stories both about the difficulty and the intense suddenness of human connection, about the profound link that exists between being in love and being alone.

**Brian Evenson,** Author of *Altmann's Tongue* and *The Wavering Knife*

Like its individual lines, the book takes us on a roller coaster ride along the peaks and nadirs of human existence, sometimes threatening to spin off the page. We get lost in the breathlessness of the language, the storm of image — to be suddenly dropped without warning, whiplashed, back to earth. Parkison somehow, magically, manages to marry the satirical wit of Donald Barthelme with the lyrical power of Anne Carson. With some Stephen Graham Jones-style horror thrown in to boot.

*Necessary Fiction*

Aimee Parkison's prose abrades, the kind of scrape on a blackboard that sends chills down the spine. One shivers long after the book is read, the reader has gone to sleep, and finds herself dreaming, not having a choice but to wake up. Though identified and published at an historical moment in U.S. history, Parkison's collection proves timeless, if not gothic.

*The Brooklyn Rail*

Aimee Parkison is a shrewd, fiery, wildly poetic, politically astute writer of fiction. Parkison gifts us with deeply imagined, and often fantastic landscapes, straight from the heart of her unique imagination, but these are always, in part, sharp commentaries on the world we have to inhabit in our daily lives. Parkison's satirical embrace, and always beautiful language, leaves you more awake to the world and unsettled in all the right ways.

**Jane McCafferty,** Author of *One Heart* and *First You Try Everything*

In Aimee Parkison's ingenious collection, words and images ricochet off the walls of the page, defying logic and gravity to expose reality's invisible footing. A kind of feminist *Tales of the Grotesque and Arabesque,* Parkison's reinvented fables, ghost tales, and murder mysteries demonstrate how absurdist extremes clear a space for the most potent polemic. Only by turning the world on its head can we see it aright: here are recognitions, simultaneously hilarious and grave.

**Mary Cappello,** Author of *Life Breaks In: A Mood Almanack*

Parkison's prose flows with a subtle, musical rhythm that only prose can achieve, and then rarely ... Every sentence, every sentence, is exquisite.

*Hayden's Ferry Review*

Aimee Parkison offers a distinct new voice to contemporary fiction. Her seductive stories explore childhood as a realm of sorrows, and reveal the afflictions of adults who emerge from this private geography

**Carol Anshaw,** Author of *Lucky in the Corner* and *Aquamarine*

Aimee Parkison's stories always surprise us, telling of the search for elusive identities, the quest for slippery selves and for what it means to be human, a woman. Her narratives lure us through many permutations of connection into a world as marvelous as it is mysterious, showing how fictions are usually truer than facts. Parkison is an exciting and memorable new voice.

**Robert Morgan,** Author of *Brave Enemies* and *Gap Creek*

Delicate, graceful, luminous, evocative ... these stories are like running a finger along a seemingly smooth edge of glass — you don't know you've been cut until you bleed.

**Cris Mazza,** Author of *Various Men Who Knew Us as Girls*

One of the most innovative fiction writers working today, Aimee Parkison never sacrifices substance for style — her electric, daring prose crackles with the compellingly messy realities of psychology, politics and sex, even in the most Surreal of moments.

**Gina Frangello,** Author of *Slut Lullabies*

# Suburban
# Death Project

# Suburban Death Project Aimee Parkison

UNBOUND EDITION PRESS

Atlanta

Copyright © 2022 by Aimee Parkison
All Rights Reserved

FIRST EDITION

Printed in the United States of America

LIBRARY OF CONGRESS RECORD

Name: Parkison, Aimee, 1976— author.
Title: Suburban Death Project / Aimee Parkison.
Edition: First edition.
Published: Atlanta : Unbound Edition Press, 2022.

LCCN: 2022930481
LCCN Permalink: https://lccn.loc.gov/2022930481
ISBN: 978-0-9913780-4-3 (hardcover)

Designed by Eleanor Safe and Joseph Floresca
Printed by Bookmobile, Minneapolis, MN
Distributed by Small Press Distribution

123456789

Unbound Edition Press
1270 Caroline Street, Suite D120
Box 448
Atlanta, GA 30307

# Contents

# Suburban Death Project

# Theatrum Insectorum

At night, Garner gazed through a magnifier at insects he considered actors. Adjusting tiny spotlights, he cherished the actors' talents. He trembled, laughed, and sighed. The insects twitched, danced, and flourished before stilling. Under the scratched lens, the living met the dead, and Garner applauded them all. Slowly, he became sentimental about preservation. He wanted to keep the best actors near him for the rest of his life.

Whenever he went into the woods to capture new recruits, he considered himself a casting agent. He took pride in his ability to discover raw talent, the hint of wings.

He left nothing to chance. While constructing stages, he cautiously selected props from the actors' natural environments. He wanted the actors to enjoy the performances. The improvised insect plays were vividly expressive and often deadly. The chorography of instinct rendered exquisite catharsis.

Garner was elderly but rarely tired as the constant catharsis offered daily renewal, energy, and wisdom. The plays continued for many decades. Ever since he was a young man, he never understood why anyone would want to watch films or television, as he considered insects to be better actors than people.

However, his delight was matched by his wife's fear of his favorite stars. Joyce flinched at every performance. Garner protectively held her hand. He tried to explain. She wouldn't listen. Mesmerizing talents became luminous on glass stages. The best actors were preserved in pillboxes in the theater of the dead.

Sometimes Joyce wept in Garner's arms because she detested the theater and its intricate glass stages.

Even after thirty-seven years of marriage, Garner never understood why Joyce admired luna moths from afar but was terrified of any insect that flew near her. While courting her, he completed his degree in entomology. He wandered into the woods and caught harmless insects to cure her entomophobia. He chased dragonflies and butterflies with nets and brought them to Joyce while they were alive and scared — longing to die or be set free. He thought if she saw how helpless they were, how much they feared her, she would escape her phobia. Foolishly, he imagined that when she realized the swallowtails would risk suicide in the nets to avoid her fingers, she would understand their vulnerability.

"Here," he used to say, "now you set them free."

Joyce lost her breath and fell, paralyzed, her silent lips pressed to the ground. Later, he learned it wasn't the stingers of the wasps or the needle beak of the mosquitoes she feared. She just never wanted the wings to touch her.

Some of Garner's favorite actors were wasps, stick insects, bees, parasol ants, nymphs, beetles, butterflies, caterpillars, larvae, hoppers, moths, flies, damselflies, and dragonflies.

He fed them nectar, leaves, flowers, rotten fruit, decaying wood, and other actors.

They took on the parts of predator and prey, moving along props and structured territories.

Carefully, Garner designed sets and stages for camouflaged colonies, and the actors revived their most celebrated roles, dancing and flying into glass walls.

✧ ✧ ✧

Mindful of Joyce's fears, Garner trapped the swallowtail in an empty mayonnaise jar as it fed off the honey on his finger.

In the small kitchen that smelled of bacon grease and cakes baking, Joyce stood at the sink with her back to Garner as she washed a green glass bowl.

Hiding the swallowtail jar, Garner felt trapped.

"Now," he said to Joyce, trying to keep his voice low so the grandchildren couldn't hear, "you just forget what I said earlier about those widows at the club."

"I never listen to your babbling," she said, drying the bowl on a small towel.

✧ ✧ ✧

The actors used their antennae for touching, picking up scents from the air. Garner admired their skill, yet he was skeptical about certain difficult personalities.

The actors led strange lives.

Sometimes, Garner had to kill them with chloroform or cyanide to preserve their structural integrity.

At other times, he ended their performances with rubbing alcohol, cleaning fluid, or ammonia.

✦ ✦ ✦

In the living room, Garner's grandson David examined the dead actors, newly deceased talents now only specimens with stiff, blue-black legs clinging to rags soaked in alcohol. David picked up one jar after another and admired the specimens slowly.

"Thanks, Gramps," David said. "This'll make a nice collection. But I need an even bigger collection to make an A on my biology project. There are only thirty here. I need at least seventy more."

"Well, okay," Garner said.

"I'll pick these up later," David said as he pointed to the insects in their jars.

As the grandchildren left, Joyce began mixing cookie dough in a large glass bowl. Her hands shook as she grasped the wooden spoon.

✦ ✦ ✦

On Sunday morning, the scent of cookies lured Garner into the kitchen. He picked up one golden-edged butter cookie from a canister on the table. For a moment, he held it to his lips.

As he bit into the cookie, he tasted something strange — something he recognized but had never encountered in his wife's baking. At first, he found the sensation elegant. Then he gagged and spat into the sink.

Examining the rest of the cookies, he discovered the black wing of a swallowtail inside. The empty jars of David's insect collection lay scattered about the kitchen. Every insect had been baked into Joyce's cookies.

Garner ate the cookies slowly, one by one, then put on a gray suit and a blue tie and left for church without Joyce.

*Why did I eat those cookies?* he thought when he entered the church and shook hands with the choir director. Then he was afraid to wonder why. The organ player began her standard song, *Jesus Saves, Jesus Saves.* If the cookies were gone, really gone, *consumed*, they might have never existed. Joyce might have never done what Garner thought she had done.

He sat with his grandchildren at the service.

"Where's Grandma?" Kaylee asked.

Garner didn't answer.

The preacher read from Proverbs: *His malice may be concealed by deception, but his wickedness will be exposed in the assembly. Like a gold ring in a pig's snout is a beautiful woman who shows no discretion. Your eyes will see strange sights and your mind imagine confusing things. Like one who takes away a garment on a cold day, or like vinegar poured on soda, is one who sings songs to a heavy heart. Better is open rebuke than hidden love. Death and Destruction are never satisfied, and neither are the eyes of man.*

After the benediction, one of the widows, a woman named Carol Century, said, "Garner, we've got something for you."

She pulled photographs out of her billfold. They were black-and-white images of six young women, naked but covered in the dark flowers they held.

"These are after our debutante ball," Betty O'Dell said, "1936. This one is me."

"They gave us red flowers with orange pollen," Beth Lessen said.

"It stuck to our noses," Carol said with a sigh muffled in her handkerchief.

Little Kaylee tugged on Garner's fingers. He looked back at the widows and tucked the photographs into his bible. He walked David and Kaylee out to his car. He felt the burden of the widow's eyes upon him as he held his grandchildren's hands.

The young actors clung to leaves and tender stems. They flitted to honey. Gently, Garner shook the stages, dislodging the hesitant along with props of leaves and rotting branches, stone, and trash.

He rearranged the sets. Everywhere were flowers. The white blossoms and red petals revived the intensity of older players. Roses seemed to provide inspiration to fresh recruits.

Living actors visited the newly dead rearranged in exquisite glass mausoleums.

"Isn't this a picture of your and Grandma's wedding?" David asked, pointing to a black-and-white photo that hung in the hallway.

Garner couldn't recognize the solemn face of the young man in the frame or the intense gaze of his bride's dark eyes.

Kaylee reached for the wedding photo. She was only four years old and couldn't understand how cruel her questions were, or so Garner thought whenever her words disturbed him.

"Why weren't you and Grandma smiling?" she asked.

"I don't know," Garner said, shaking his head. "It was a long time ago."

✧ ✧ ✧

In his driveway, Garner looked up to the clouded sky. He felt guilty, knowing he shouldn't have left Joyce. For more than three decades, they had been going to church together. But since she couldn't get out of bed that morning and didn't seem right, he decided to let her rest. That was why he went without her.

Silently, he entered the house.

"Bring me some ice," Joyce whispered.

He brought a pitcher of ice and handed her a single cube wrapped in a cloth. She rubbed it over her lips.

"My mouth is dry," she said apologetically.

He walked to the other side of the bed and lay down beside her for the first time in over twenty years. She gave him a frightened look. He couldn't blame her. All he remembered of their new marriage was clumsy touches in the dark, robes that hid her ankles, the closed yellow diary, the locked bathroom where the walls were doused with perfume and candle fumes rose, her back turned to him as she nursed their son, Howard, who became a medical supplies salesman.

"Have you seen Howard?" Joyce asked.

"He's in Wichita." Garner stroked her soft frail arms, hairless and exceedingly pale, ladylike. Decades ago, she began singeing the hairs on her forearms. She had been striking matches ever since.

"Would you bring me that yellow date book off the shelf?" she asked.

"Do you know the difference between a date book and a diary?" Garner asked as he slid his index finger over the ribbon he never dared to untie.

"Don't start."

"I've got something to show you," Garner said.

He pulled the photos of the debutantes out of his bible and handed them to Joyce.

"Why?" Joyce asked. She opened the yellow book and threw it on Garner's lap.

Expecting details of her fantasy life lining the pages, he read it and was surprised to find only recipes and records of birthdays long past. For almost week, Garner kept going back to Joyce's yellow book, flipping through its pages, searching for anything he might not have known about her. He found no secrets, nothing unusual in what she had written.

The grandchildren began to stay away from her. Joyce asked Garner to cut spidery fingers off the walls, to mend holes above her head, and to tear black webs from the corners when all he saw were the bare walls and the white painted ceiling above her.

"I know if you'd just win that golf tournament everything would be all right. If you'd just play and win, I could get well," she said.

"What tournament?" he asked.

She looked at him with disgust.

At night, there was always drama on the screens of the lighted theaters where nocturnal actors played. The lamps and spotlights created a fury of activity.

Actors fluttered and danced, flying and hanging upside-down. They celebrated, drunk on light.

Later, Garner would slowly dissect them in pillboxes. With each dawn dissection, he marveled over the toughness of the exoskeleton, the softness of the organs, and the actors' colorless blood.

Three days later, the sound of Garner's golf shoes on the muddy green reminded him of a song certain actors sang. He hummed, hands sweeping in the sharp, rhythmical gestures of the choir director he had watched last Sunday. A dragonfly landed on his sleeve, and he stopped his song to predict which way it would travel.

Garner walked into the clubhouse with a handful of quarters. The wives of his dead golf partners beckoned to him. Old age seemed to enlarge the widows, their breasts spilling beneath their soft arms, billowing under their sleeves. But time had devoured Joyce, transforming her from a delicate girl to a bone-thin, bone-tired woman. Day by day, he watched the light fade from her eyes.

Garner ignored the lines of the widows' thick bras and panties showing through the rough, synthetic fabric — pink, green, red, and yellow — of their lawn clothes. The widows' soft, sagging flesh stayed firmly in place with the aid of rigid wired undergarments — some he could imagine, but most so scientific, so painfully complex he was too tired to dream of them.

All six women sat on worn, gold-felt couches in front of the windows.

"How's Joyce getting along?" Betty asked.

Garner looked hesitantly out the window and studied the empty cart.

✛ ✛ ✛

At home, Joyce was still resting in bed. "What you got there, Mister?" she asked.

He handed her a sandwich, placing it on her lap.

"Why don't you eat?" he asked.

"Not hungry," she said.

"Eat."

"Betty has put on a little weight, don't you think?"

"A little meat on the bones never did any harm. It's not a bad thing for a woman to have on her when she gets older," he said.

"My stars!"

"Whatever it is that's ailing you, you're just determined to hurry it along, aren't you?" He felt angry and didn't know why. He loved her, yet he had never said as much. Neither had she.

✛ ✛ ✛

Even though Garner knew Joyce was dying, he longed for the woods where the actors gathered. He grabbed a net and ran. In the last hours of her life, he captured dragonflies and butterflies. He pulled ladybugs out of the lettuce garden by the hundreds. He pulled red wasps from the trees and held on to their black wings without being stung. He flushed baby grasshoppers from the weeds and found locusts still wet and clinging to their shells. He held the spindle-backed bloodsucker and never felt its bite. He placed insects inside glass jars and brought them into the house.

With great care — ingenuity, really — Garner constructed a fountain and a miniature garden under glass. He designed the misty water stage for a solitary emperor dragonfly.

The male emperor kept watch over his territory, able to fly for many hours without rest. He was blue like a sapphire and lovelier. He darted. His wings were supported by tough veins.

"Don't die," Garner said to the new actors. "I don't want to be alone."

One by one, he opened the jars and released the woodland actors onto their tiny stages. They hesitated during the first moments and then flew out of the jars as if embracing their good fortune only to panic. For a while, the humming of dragonfly wings competed with the dull plunk of beetles flying into glass walls.

# Joe and Irish

I once dated an anthropologist. He committed suicide three days after
my twenty-fifth birthday. He wrote one massive book on the history
of humor in parenting practices of early hominids and primates, along
with comparisons to post-colonial times, including the use of jokes,
especially practical, to teach children to overcome the fear of death.
His mother, who outlived him by more than thirty years, was the only
family he had, the rest having gone to early graves, since suicide ran
in his mother's family and he had never met his father. His mother
was a lovely woman, bohemian, and young for her age, the sort of lithe
woman people used to call "feisty," a former professional ballerina who
had kept her figure, even after raising her son while a single mother.
As much as I loved him, I admired her greatly and wanted to be her
friend. Something changed, though, when he asked me to marry him.
Something wasn't quite right between us.

She didn't like to wear clothes indoors. This took some getting
used to. All fake red hair and beige underwear, she hosted a small
birthday party for me when I turned twenty-five. Offering to cook
dinner, she invited me and her son to celebrate the evening in a
house full of candles and cocktails gleaming. She gifted me a large,
high-end bright blue lapis vibrator, realistically sculpted, a phallus
to die for. Its impressive meandering veins trailed tip to shaft,
heartbreakingly uncut and paradoxically poetic. Beautiful, obviously
expensive, custom made, it was deliciously inappropriate to the point
of being touchingly passive aggressive. I held the vibrator in my hand,
impressed by its massive girth, having all the discretion of a sudden
nosebleed joshing from a deviated septum. It was the kind of gift that
told me the giver both loved me deeply and hated my guts. It was

the thought that counted. I felt closer to her in that moment than I ever had to my own mother, because I realized how important I had become to her, more important than she ever wanted me to be.

I was the love of her only son's life. He was perhaps the love of hers, even though he didn't know it. The vibrator should have been a clue to how much she loved him, but he didn't see it that way. I did. Everything that happened that night was because of how much she loved him.

"I don't know what to make of this," the anthropologist said to his mother as I caressed the vibrator like a baby kitten in my lap. He stood near me in the living room, beside the iron staircase that went up to his childhood bedroom and playroom. In the silence, I stared at the living room windows, the faded beige curtains bellowing in the breeze so they resembled old wedding dresses worn by pregnant brides. Headless brides, I thought.

She was smiling too much, her exquisitely painted eyebrows black as asphalt as she laughed. "I didn't mean anything by it. I just thought it was nice, something I would have appreciated at that age."

"Jesus, Mom," he said as she lit more candles and then drained her Cosmo, her fiery red curls stiff and gleaming.

I felt uncomfortable, staring at her underwear, her small firm breasts still sitting high as prized peaches stacked on shelves, the muscles working in her slender legs. Her skin, milk-glass, luminous.

"I hope you're not upset with me, son?"

"Of course, not, Mother," he said, kissing her rouged cheek.

"Well, I'll just light a few more candles, then I'll make us some more cocktails and prepare dinner."

"Lovely," I said, still clutching the vibrator, not knowing where to put it. If I put it down too fast, I would seem ungrateful or prudish, so I held it, making sure they both knew I wasn't squeamish or uncomfortable.

"What are we having?" the anthropologist asked.

"What do you mean?" his mother asked

"For dinner?"

"I don't think I like your tone, son."

"Well, don't let that spoil Carla's birthday."

"I said I was sorry."

"No, Mom."

She picked up our glasses and rushed into the kitchen. He wouldn't even glance my way, as we both sat in the living room, waiting. Soon, a loud, jarring whirring sound came from the kitchen, a grating hum and then the sound of popping. "What the hell?" he asked. His eyes radiated something I had never seen in him: a pronounced sadness, like giving up.

His mother, still in her underwear, waltzed into the dining room with a big bowl of popcorn and then rushed back to the kitchen for cocktails. "Dinner," she said, "is served."

Distracted, I laid my lapis vibrator on the table and chose a seat.

I filled my bowl happily and began munching popcorn while sipping my Cosmo.

"What's wrong, son?" she asked. "This used to be your favorite dinner."

I thought it wrong for him to refuse the popcorn, so I began eating more and more, stuffing it into my mouth as fast as I could.

"When I was five," he said.

"Well." She popped a piece of popcorn into her mouth and chewed pointedly.

"I'm not a kid anymore. I've grown out of everything I used to do when I was five."

"Everything?"

"Everything!"

"Do you remember Joe and Irish?"

"No."

"You do?"

"Stop it, Mother."

"Irish," she called loudly, her voice directed at the ceiling, as if calling someone upstairs, where his old bedroom and playroom were.

"Joe?"

"Mother!"

"Let's go. Upstairs, son. Come on, let's go see Irish and Joe."

"I said stop."

"So, you remember?"

"No!" he yelled.

"If you don't remember, what are you afraid of?"

"I'm not."

"Then, come on, get your drink, and let's go upstairs, to your old room."

He lifted his glass and chugged it, draining the Cosmo before shattering the glass on the table. She laughed and started to run, pausing at the foot of the stairs to glance back at him. He started to run after her, chasing her up the old stairs and she was laughing.

More laughter, harder, louder from her, but he was screaming at her, angrier than I'd ever known him to be. Behind his anger, I sensed fear. Maybe that's why I stopped and just stood there, listening to them and looking up. She was still laughing so hard, like a naughty little girl and he was scolding her, fatherly, but his voice was trembling, breaking.

Then, I heard other sounds — a thud, a crash, objects thrown at the walls, and she began to howl. I heard her weeping softly as he walked down the stairs, slowly, as if embarrassed, straightening his mussed hair and glasses. I saw her naked legs run past the stair landing above as he was putting on his coat to leave, saying to me, "Come on, Carla."

He gestured to me to hurry, holding the front door open when she began calling, mocking him, saying "Stop it, stop it, Mom!" Then, "See, you never grew out of it."

The anthropologist drove me home that night without a word, but I knew something had changed between us and would never be the same.

We never married. I never saw or heard from him again.

Three days after the incident, he died.

His mother asked me not to attend his funeral.

When I finally visited his grave, it was covered with white petals. I didn't have any flowers, so I removed the blue vibrator from my handbag and nestled it among the blooms others left.

The anthropologist's grave was sandwiched between two older graves in a family section, one belonging to a man named Irish, one to a man named Joe.

It was just a game, his mother later said, when I called to tell her what I thought of her. Just a game they played, she insisted, since there were only two plots left for her and her son in the family section. They knew the names of the men they would be buried next to, their neighbors for eternity, names they had known since childhood.

Do you remember a man named Irish, a man named Joe? Velvet, the shelves covered in dust on those days of the storybook Irish was reading with his eyes closed because he did not want to let me be lonely. Now, the tree outside the window, the specter. When we were children, we sometimes let our imaginations get the best of us. We scared each other. On accident. Never on purpose. Don't tell me it hasn't haunted you all these years. The shelves, the velvet dust beneath something sparkling, your eyes.

# Abandoned Nest

From Rick's ragged whispers in the dark, I gathered the man who once lived inside the foreclosure had been injured in a motorcycle accident one misty and wet summer night. On rainy nights, Tennessee highways were more dangerous than live wires. I assumed the loss of his house had something to do with the accident. Apparently, he had a young wife and twin daughters. Although they were gone before Rick and I moved into the neighborhood, I often wondered why the empty house stood neglected, personal possessions left inside the rooms.

Our neighbors became trespassers, breaking into the unoccupied house in broad daylight, but I couldn't risk confronting them.

I imagined droppings across the floor, warped doorframes, a skittering in my mind. Having majored in architecture, I knew one house could mean different things to different people. As carpenter ants reshaped rotted wood, architecture wasn't just design but memory, context, opportunity. Even in the best neighborhoods, even in the worst, fate was the architect of all foreclosures. Because of a tragic accident, squirrels became lucky as humans suffered. Time, like space, was a harbinger of design: abandoned nests under eves, animals crawling through dead leaves.

Trespassers lugged bulky items through shadowy spaces, congregating in the sitting room where squirrels darted in and out of broken windows. Watching them, I realized tragedies happen because damage is the brainchild of discovery. Disrepair has a design all its own. Even now, I see it best in abandoned spaces used for unintended purposes. I didn't know it then, but I know it now: violence is an art form. Trespassers reinvent houses they enter in the way criminals transform victims who survive violent crimes.

This, too, is architecture.

This is — or was — a neighborhood. My neighborhood, the neighborhood of the motorcycle man.

The gate remained unlocked, as did the sliding glass door to the backyard. The bank seemed to have lost interest in the property, which the manager and inspectors rarely visited. It was hard to watch the trespassers, to pretend not to see people going in and out, freely, carrying items out of the back doors — a toy church organ, a projector, dishes, a bicycle, an oven, a dishwasher, a guitar.

Even though it was a victimless crime, I said, "It isn't right."

"Why?" Rick asked.

The neighbors were plundering, getting away with it, while I watched and got nothing.

Rick kissed me in the morning. I watched squirrels in the windows. Dirty windows.

"They are vandals," I said, "all of them, especially the squirrels." They were prowling behind barred windows, staring me down from the other side of the glass.

"No more squirrel patrol," Rick said.

"But they're there, inside the house," I whispered, imagining squirrels running through the rooms. Were they trapped inside?

On my days off, I explored the neighborhood alone. When walking, I sometimes felt someone watching me, but there were so many trees growing so close together along the trail it was hard to know for certain. The squirrels? Eventually, I saw one of the boys from the local high school, Billy Teller. Long, tall, brooding, Billy wore faded jeans and a ripped t-shirt stained with a V of sweat. He smelled sweet, beery so bees flocked to him on the wooded trails.

"What you're doing isn't right." He lit a cigarette and walked away into the trees, where another high school boy, Abraham Jones, stood watching. The boys disappeared in vines encircling trees surrounded by overgrown shrubs.

Nearing my house, I studied fallen branches dangling from power lines and phone lines. Squirrels leapt onto roofs, chewing rotten wood beneath damaged shingles. I felt as if Billy or Abraham were still watching, following me, but I couldn't see them. The dense trees and brush along the creek trail behind the houses hid so much.

Because the neighborhood had been built over an old pecan grove, nuts fell every year, keeping the squirrels exuberant as they gazed into the windows of houses nearest their favorite trees. Whenever I walked out onto the balcony, I heard rustling in the leaves. And another sound: cracking and thudding. I assumed this was the breaking and falling of branches to the ground.

"Hidden," Rick said, as I stared at the two boys, whom Rick simply ignored, "by dirt and leaves."

I thought of how the vines and the new leaves had begun to hide even the trespassers who entered the damaged sliding glass panel of the back door. The squirrels, too, had begun to re-enter the foreclosure, gnawing through the rotted roof.

Rick reclaimed materials from the scrap pile: branches fallen from a large pecan tree between the houses, a long-sanded board, eye bolts, rope. Rick climbed the tree and hung the swing from a sturdy branch near our bedroom window. In this pecan tree, barred owls roosted.

"The motorcycle man," Rick said, "was a professor."

"And he died?"

Rick didn't answer.

Smiling, I grabbed the rope and looked up at the owls' nest. I wanted to swing through the night as the owls called to each other during mating season. Addicted to the simple pleasure I once thought lost to childhood, I swung under the shadow of pecans for hours.

Watching the squirrels in the windows as they watched me, I peered into the house and realized the curtains had been stripped.

"Who's that?" I asked, seeing a man walking inside the house and surveying its contents.

"The investor," Rick said, "just bought it for a song."

As I swung over the next several days, the investor escorted buyers through the rooms. I assumed they were collectors and shop owners. They seemed to appraise items, handling the professor's possessions as if to assess their value and quality.

The people who lived in the house before the squirrels must have been packrats. Or hoarders. How else could there be so many items left to sell after so much had been stolen?

I watched in disbelief, unseen in the pecan trees' shadows, or so I thought. The investor sold china, wine glasses, antiques, framed art, photographs, books, wooden furniture, cutlery, and jewelry. Even a pair of mountain bikes. A striped humpback sofa, an art deco waterfall bed set, Asian folding screens, and mirrors were carried by crews of movers. Big, sweaty men hoisted cumbersome items onto an unmarked truck. They lifted pedestals, a wine bar, and an entertainment center complete with a bridge piece connecting two pier cabinets. Later, a truck marked "antiques" hauled away a mid-century king set and queen set, a mid-century Haywood & Wakefield kneehole desk, and a set of four Tommy Bahama-style armchairs.

I ached with longing for the library of old books that remained, the cream reading chair and matching ottoman, the pine dresser with chest and nightstand. I coveted the oak electric fireplace, the sleeper sofa with its air mattress, the rocker, and the tall chest — even if they were all covered with scratches and squirrel droppings.

An elderly woman, maybe the investor's mother, ordered men to load her pickup truck: jewelry boxes, chandeliers, clocks, mirrors, Persian and Oriental rugs, and a mid-century dinette.

What caught my attention most was displayed on the house's front yard. In overgrown grass, near the untrimmed hedges, rested an antique mule trunk, a pair of upholstered armchairs, and a lovely pewter-leaf mirror. I felt these items belonged inside my house, even if I couldn't afford to buy them and even if they were gnawed by rodent teeth. Squirrels, like most rodents, were always chewing because their teeth were always growing.

Behind the windows, the investor gestured wildly as buyers at the private estate sale touched and examined items. I peered inside, straining my eyes, and was surprised to catch glimpses of Rick inside the house with the squirrels. Once the buyers left, the workmen began to clear the remaining contents, taking truckloads of damaged goods and paperwork, probably to the local dump. As I swung, I watched my husband walking behind the windows with the investor.

Rick began to move the furniture from the grass into our house. When I asked him how he managed to haggle for the items, he only kissed me the way he always kissed me, softly at first but then harder. His stubble began to hurt me, burning my face until I opened my mouth. He sucked the air out of me and then forced his breath into me. In those early years of marriage, for some reason, CPR was foreplay. That meant something. I just never knew what.

The following nights I was awakened by an engine, a motorcycle revving, racing through the neighborhood streets. My husband was missing from our bedroom. In the dark, the sound of the motorcycle cruising so close by, repeatedly, gave me chills. I thought of the empty house.

I almost never asked questions about the motorcycle, which my husband began driving at night and parking in our carport during the day. Perhaps because I was so pleased with the furniture, when it came to the motorcycle, I waited for my husband to tell me what he wanted me to know.

When I went outside, entering the carport the next morning, I found a dead squirrel beside the driver's side door of our old car. The squirrel was just lying there on the concrete, no marks on it, fat and healthy and perfect looking, eyes wide open. Only one thing seemed to be wrong: its tail was gone. It didn't seem to have been raggedly torn or bitten off. It had been cut clean from the body. Gone.

When Rick began riding the motorcycle, I began substitute teaching at the local high school, where Billy Teller and Abraham Jones were students. Since my oldest students were not that much younger than I, being mistaken for a student walking the high-school halls was not uncommon. Rick was doing lots of odd jobs in those days, mostly welding and construction. A handyman and a private contractor, Rick always seemed busy working for the investor, and I became lonely. I began talking to Abraham after school and between classes as Billy watched from a distance.

Each weekday morning, I woke early, waiting for a call from the high school. As a new substitute teacher, I was eager to work. I made myself available, even at the last minute. I wanted to teach every day. On the days I walked to work, Abraham Jones often walked with me, but his friend Billy Teller did not.

"You've seen people going in and out of the house?" Abraham asked. I pretended I hadn't known his parents were among the trespassers. His family lived in a large brick ranch-style house up the street from my house, four houses up from the house on the right.

"And squirrels," I said.

Long dark curls fell over his deep-set brown eyes, hiding one eye completely. With his sweet smile and bright teeth, he was the type of boy I would have had a crush on, when I was still in high school, less than five years before I met him.

His face was beautiful before Billy ruined it.

Like Abraham, Billy had been suspended for two weeks because of the fight. Unlike Abraham, Billy never returned to school after his suspension ended.

"Probably dropped out," the principal later said. "For the best, really."

I agreed.

When Abraham walked back home with me, I decided to ask about Billy, one more time, just to make sure he was gone.

"Mind if I walk with you, again?" Abraham asked.

I liked the company and knew he would never tell anyone what happened. I remembered waking on the bathroom tile, shivering, stunned as he helped me stand.

"Keep an eye on Abraham," the principal, Mr. Peters, had said to me after the fight between Billy and Abraham. "I know he considers you a friend. He's a good boy. You might be able to save him before he becomes another Billy Teller."

At night, alone on my swing, I saw Billy watching me through a window, hiding in the vacant house.

I couldn't tell Rick because I feared he might kill Billy after guessing what he had done.

I had no visible injuries. Without injuries, there was no proof. I couldn't talk to Rick. I couldn't tell the school. Too many female teachers had been arrested, jailed, and exposed on television for having sex with students.

What if people thought I wanted it to happen?

What if he did it again and claimed we were dating?

What if I had to register as a sex offender, even though I was the victim?

I was the adult and he was the child, my student, but that didn't remove his power over me.

Abraham spent a day at the hospital and then his family kept him inside his house, grounded, his bruised face healing.

When Abraham visited me later, he said, "I used to know him."

"Who?" I asked, worried he meant my husband.

"Jarred Plano, the guy who lived in that house." Abraham pointed to the foreclosure, the house on the left. "He had two daughters. And a wife, Laney. A beautiful woman I used to swing with. So did Billy. He had a motorcycle."

Just then, my husband's truck pulled into the driveway. I told Abraham he had to go.

Abraham walked away, but when he neared the house on the left, he stopped, looked back, and said, "Who put that back?"

"What?" I asked.

"The swing."

"What do you mean?"

"It was here before."

Abraham walked across the yard to the swing and bent over to examine the seat, the eyebolts, and the ropes.

That evening, I fried an entire package of bacon. Slicing three tomatoes, I prepared BLT sandwiches for dinner, Rick's favorite food, to put him in a good mood.

"Lots of mayo," he said. "Not too much lettuce. Make that bacon crispy."

"Yes, sir," I said.

"Tomatoes sliced thinly?" he asked.

Even though he loved these sandwiches, there were things that could ruin them for him: stingy mayonnaise, excessive lettuce, soggy bacon, and thick tomato slices. I made sure that I always prepared the sandwiches to his liking, especially that evening when I needed answers.

"Terrific," Rick said, sitting down at the table with its plastic covering.

"I've really been enjoying my swing," I said.

"Great."

"How did you ever think to put a swing there, anyway?"

"Why?"

"It's such a perfect place for a swing, really on the very edge of the property. How did you think to put it there, of all places?"

He took a bite, chewing carefully. "Let me think."

"Where did you get the swing, Rick?"

"What?"

Reaching for another sandwich, studying it carefully, he put it down on his plate. "What?"

"Someone told me that swing used to be here, before we moved here."

"That kid from the school? The one who's got a fucked up face and is always following you around? What happened to him, anyway?"

"He said ours is the same swing that was there before, that you just put it back where it was."

"Is that a crime?"

I began to wonder. Then, I started to wonder if it was wrong to keep secrets from my husband. What good did it do to report crimes? The neighborhood was a living thing. Every assault altered the landscape. Quiet could protect it.

"Why didn't you tell me?"

"Why would I?"

Later that night, when we were in bed and I was pretending to sleep, I sensed Rick watching me.

He whispered, "Something's wrong."

"Nothing's wrong."

"You used to talk to me."

"Do you expect me to tell you everything?"

"What happened? What's wrong?"

"Leave me alone."

When he reached for the light switch, I stilled his hand.

He slowly rose from the bed and began dressing in the dark. I heard him put on his boots and then walk down the stairs and out the front door. I heard the motorcycle engine rev as it sped away. I waited.

Rising from the bed, I slipped on my robe and sandals before exiting the house through the back door. I snuck behind the trees near the creek, where a woman with long dark hair was swinging in my swing.

When I heard the motorcycle approaching, I hid behind the trees. Rick parked in the driveway of the professor's house. He walked toward the front door and moved into an area blocked from my view. The next thing I knew, I saw him through the lit windows. Rick was inside the house, talking to the investor. He gestured wildly with his hands and the investor took notes on a clipboard. By now, the house had been gutted, the squirrels evicted by exterminators, everything of value sold and carted away. All the trash — gnawed and tattered rugs, molded plush furniture, and a hammock — had been stacked on the exterior brick walls near the old charcoal grill and some dismantled shelving. Rick motioned toward the ceiling, the walls, and finally toward the windows.

The woman in the swing stopped. Innocent faces frozen in fear, uncertainty, or perhaps surprise, twin girls stood behind her. They did not utter a sound, and turned to look at me. An infant began to wail.

"Who's there?" the woman asked, turning the ropes, twirling around in the swing. She now faced me but perhaps couldn't see me well enough in the dark to distinguish my features.

"Rick's wife," I said, stepping out of the tree shadows and into the moonlight. "You know him?"

"We used to live in the other house."

"The motorcycle man's house?" I asked, before realizing how callous and stupid the question sounded.

"He's going to be all right, but I've been feeling strangely ever since our baby was born," the woman said, gazing at me. "I keep thinking about the swing. I want to rock my baby in my swing. It helps. Did Rick tell you?"

"What?"

"I shouldn't have come back."

"You can swing here anytime. You don't have to sneak around."

"There was something wrong with Billy, wasn't there?" She rose from the swing before leading the twins away. "I want to go back. But I'm afraid of Billy. He's still here, isn't he?"

After that night, Rick informed me that he and Billy had begun working for the investor full time. Rick became the investor's right-hand man and Billy became Rick's, the two overseeing various renovation projects throughout town. When the investor bought another foreclosure in the neighborhood, they began remodeling it as well. Together, they painted over trespassers' fingerprints across abandoned houses, creating homes for new neighbors who had never known the old.

# The Ambassador Owl

Jefferson, Texas, on a sticky spring afternoon, I wait for disaster to rain down like tiny frogs clinging to branches after a tornado. My husband Jace, a heavy man, dons a faded tractor hat. Shielding his eyes from the sun, he steers his motorized wheelchair down the ramp outside our house while whistling "Don't Worry, Be Happy."

Closing the door behind him, I slide the window open and pop off the screen. A blast of hot, muggy air hits my face like breath. Outside, baby grasshoppers jump like hot oil on a griddle. Robins sing. Owls hoot. The sky ebbs the deep vivid blue of painted china.

Meanwhile, I pretend I'm cleaning the windows so I can watch Jace. Something is different with him lately. These past few weeks, I've caught him doing things he's not supposed to be doing. When he first started using the wheelchair, the doctors told us certain actions might not be possible. I wonder how it's possible for him to get in and out of our bed these days without using the rails? He never mentions it, never even acknowledges what's happening.

We've been living here for two years, ever since our retirement from the military, and we're accustomed to a life of lakes and tourists, friendly dog walkers. Our lot is surrounded by trees and owls. Big pickup trucks hauling shiny fishing boats on trailers cruise by our oversize carport, slowing down to view the stretch of asphalt where Jace's neglected pontoon boat and bass boat sit, gathering cobwebs beneath the oaks. At this hour, the dense shade of mature maples bathes the ramps near the end of the driveway. Standing near the window, hidden by umber curtains, I spy on Jace, my husband of ten years, a diabetic and avid fisherman who has stopped going near the water. Lately he's become focused on the sky.

He lost his legs to nerve damage last summer.

Now that he's disabled, I'm constantly spying, keeping watch, to search and inspect his body, the house, the wheelchair, our surroundings, looking for clues that we'll be alright. Once a birder addicted to owling, I observe without disturbance, though I don't go birding or owling anymore.

Long before Jace, my first love was the monkey-faced owl, a barn owl that roosted near my childhood home. I remember its humanlike face, the eyes directed forward, the wide wings, and hooked beak. I listened for the strange, loud double-clicking echoes among buildings and the screaming. Searching for its droll, quizzical expression and white underparts reflected in streetlights, I loved that owl. I fell for it, the way I would eventually fall for men who were strangers to me. When I gave myself to them, the men reminded me of owls, their quizzical expressions, white bellies, their secretive nature. I stalked them, when I was young, but only the secretive ones.

Nearing the end of the cracked concrete drive, the wheelchair stalls. Jace jerks back, as if realizing he is on display. He halts the chair at the final stretch, just before the asphalt road. I hold my breath, wondering if he'll be able to reach far enough to get the newspaper. It's right there on the concrete, wrapped in its clear plastic bag, where the carrier threw it.

The neighbors are watching. I spy them in their windows, looking out, on their front porches, in their yards, pretending to tend to the grass. Yesterday, this moment birthed disaster. A little thing like a man going out to retrieve the newspaper on his own driveway. Yesterday, Jace had fallen out of his chair. Hard. Smacked to the concrete. His hands and elbows and face were bleeding. Bruises all over his pale skin. I ran out of the house to lift him back into his wheelchair. He was too heavy. The neighbors ran to gather him in their arms, picking him up and putting him back into his chair.

"Okay," he said, smiling but shaking. "Don't worry. I'm fine."

Inside the house, I cleaned his wounds with iodine and checked for broken bones before laying ice packs on his elbows.

Today, just as he's bending down, grasping, Jace removes a metal pen from his shirt pocket in a flourish. He flicks this pen, which has a pointer, retractable and approximately two and a half feet long at full length. He nudges the paper with it. He thumbs the end of the pointer, and a claw on the opposite end flexes outward, grabbing the newspaper. Jace lifts the paper, hanging from the end of the pointer, into the air. The neighbors watching from their porches applaud.

Jace smiles and waves at everyone, before turning his wheelchair back to the ramps.

He's a clever man, my husband, with unusual charm, the ability to disarm even his greatest detractors, like his mother-in-law, who never liked me being with Jace, who is nearly my father's age. I always preferred older men. I remember what Mother said when she found out I was marrying Jace: *A fisherman is a jerk on one end of the line waiting for a jerk on the other.* Jace laughed about that for days, but I didn't think it funny.

"An old fisherman lives here with the catch of his life," he announced to Mother when she first visited this house, shortly before his amputations.

Mother only smiled wryly, asking for a drink, then whispering in the kitchen, "The fishing is always better on the other side of the lake, isn't it, dear?"

I didn't know what she meant.

"There's something fishy about this fella," she said after a few drinks, while eyeing all the prize-winning bass mounted on the den walls near Jace's trophies.

"I'll not deny it," said Jace.

This was before he lost his legs, when he went fishing every weekend, rain or shine, and won competition trophies.

"Early to bed, early to rise, fish all day, make up lies?" Mother asked, examining his trophies.

Mother's mention of "lies" and "rise" unnerved me for reasons I only began to understand later.

Jace raised an eyebrow and his beer to her. "You know the old proverb, Norma? Give a man a fish, and he will eat for a day ... Teach a man to fish, and he will sit in a boat, and drink beer all day."

"Men and fish are alike," Mother said to me later that night before turning into bed. "They both get into trouble when they open their mouths."

Jace was so deliciously sunburned.

He smelled of the lake, the wind, the sun, the water.

He tasted sun-kissed.

His hairdo was courtesy of his boat, in the days when he used to assure me that I could separate the men from the boys by the size of their rods.

That was before the amputations, when Jace lived to fish and fished to live, when life was too short to fish without beer. Back when wishes were fishes and everyday was a fish fry, Jace used to live for the lake, the water, the catch of the day. So strong, determined, adventurous, full of energy, before his amputations, he was the one who carried me to bed when I was tired. Now, I spend hours regretting I'm not strong enough to carry him.

I used to venture out at night to go owling. He used to leave for the lake in the dark hours of morning so that we crossed each other in our adventures, one of us coming home, one of us leaving. Now, we both stay at home. He resents it, though not as much as my asking why he doesn't go to the lake anymore. There are other things we don't do anymore, but I don't like to think about them.

Sometimes at night, I venture into the yard to stand beside the decaying pontoon boat. That's how I first saw the neighborhood ambassador owl and realized the owl was calling to me, letting itself be known as owls rarely do. I wanted to explain to the owl it was too late for me. I no longer went on trips to search for nests in caves, tree hollows, bridges, and buildings. Gone were my childhood visits to caves littered with droppings, pellets scattered amid golden-brown feathers.

The owls I once loved fed on cotton rats and nested in deserted buildings, bridges, and water towers, never during the years of rodent shortage. They refused to brood in hunger. The mated pair I watched for months fed their brood on the foreparts of rats, leaving hind parts and separate stomachs scattered around the nest. I found them by searching for scattered stomachs of rats they killed.

Tonight, the bold ambassador owl finds me, again, and stares with inquisitive eyes. He's a barn owl with the perfect white monkey face.

The owl and I stare at each other near the carport where the pontoon boat rusts in the dust of neglect. I notice one of the owl's wings is damaged, wounded, and I wonder if it knows what Jace and I have learned. A body can become a stranger, a separate entity that abandons the self and its lovers. I feel guilty about not noticing this sooner, though I was the one to spot the sores. The trouble began on Jace's left foot, an ulcer that wouldn't heal.

What happened to Jace was related to his diabetes, but the official medical reason for his amputations was poor circulation due to damage to his arteries. Without adequate blood flow, the body's cells cannot get oxygen and nutrients they need. Infections do not go away or cannot be controlled. With so much resulting nerve damage to his feet, Jace couldn't feel pain. This meant he couldn't heal. He had an ulcer on his foot that grew and became infected, but he never even felt it or knew it was there until I discovered it.

Jace isn't the only one who can't feel pain. Some people stare at amputees, regardless of what they are doing, never realizing the pain they are causing. I guess to some people pain is interesting. Watching struggle is entertainment.

"I'm a free show," Jace says, whenever we catch people staring at him.

"I'll never forgive them," I whisper, especially when those staring are adults.

He tells me he no longer takes it personally.

"Everyone needs to invent a new game or to find a game to make life worth living, or else we die," he says. "Staring at me is just a game to them."

I'm thinking how wise he is, how much sense his words make, but how little his wisdom relates to his actions. His game was once fishing. Is he inventing a new game, testing its rules? I wonder if he isn't following his own advice or if he has a secret game he hasn't revealed to me.

Tonight, as I walk out of the house, quietly, wanting to be alone with the full moon, just for a little while, not daring to go beyond the confines of our property, I end up walking to the pontoon boat. I stroke the dust on the paint and remember the sun on the water.

I wonder when the ambassador owl will return. It blends into the bark of the trees, never revealing its roost, even after crows mobbing. Unlike the Romans, I don't believe owl hoots signal death. Like the Greeks, I feel hoots as good fortune.

"I've seen it before," Jace says, when I go back inside the house, where he's waiting for me near the fireplace full of lit candles. "I know what you're doing."

"What?" I ask.

"Your friend in the trees? He watches me too, and I have plans for him."

"What do you mean?" I'm worried for the owl.

When Jace tells me what he plans to do with the ambassador owl, I begin to wonder, if it works, will it be because of the strangeness of the wounded owl or that of my husband?

✛ ✛ ✛

The next day, Jace gets to work on his new game, taking a full week to prepare. I try to watch from the windows, but he waits until I'm not looking before doing anything. He only gets things done when I'm not watching. Somehow, he rigs a system of ropes, weights, and wheels, fashioning long pulleys behind our house, cords stretching from tree to tree to hang homemade wooden cages dangling like chandeliers from heavy branches. Somehow, he installs huge, high-powered spotlights to shine on the night sky. The neighbors watch from their back porches, mesmerized. I wonder: *what have they seen?*

We have an entire neighborhood of "concerned" citizens who can't keep their eyes off Jace. I hide my outrage. What good would it do? He's drawing attention to himself, making everyone stare even more, giving them an excuse.

Jace, gleeful, says, "It's all part of the new sport I've invented." He appears proud people are watching. "They're taking pictures and making videos, honey," he says.

The neighbors have invited friends to watch him. Local tourists have gotten word, driving by our house slowly to get a glimpse of Jace and the system he has rigged in the backyard, the mystery he has created. Jace won't tell anyone what he's really doing. I pretend to be enthusiastic because it has been a long time since I've seen him this way.

"Bless your little heart," Jace says, when I tell him I'm worried.

His spirits are lifted, his eyes are full of light like on days of fishing tournaments. The neighbors, gazing shamelessly, cheer him. He's a local sensation, a freak.

✛ ✛ ✛

Only in Jefferson, I think. A former fisherman, Jace is just the type of man for this place. So much of his spectacle is possible because Jefferson is located between Caddo Lake and Lake O' the Pines. It thrives on tourists who visit for outdoor recreational activities and events every year, like the Holiday Light Trail and the Barbecue Cook-Off. Jefferson is ripe for a new event, a new sensation, the sort of nightly sideshow Jace is creating. Here, we have many nature activities, including steam paddleboat lake tours, horse-drawn carriage rides, antique shops, ghost tours, and now Jace.

Maybe that's why no one has called the police yet. No one has reported Jace because people are looking forward to more spectacle. Friends and strangers gather around our fence in the evening to watch and chat. As Jace moves in circles across the oversized balcony and down the ramps into our gently slopped backyard, he's holding a fishing pole. The fishing line whips through the air over the trees, and the new sport he has invented seems like a crime against nature.

"Jace," I say, "explain to me what you think you're doing?"

"Fishing for owls," he announces.

The dozen or so spectators who have gathered around our chain-link fence applaud and he asks them politely to please turn off their cameras.

"What?" I whisper.

"If I can fish from the lake, I can fish from the sky," Jace says.

No matter how many times I beg him not to, no matter how I try to reason with him, he's determined to fish for owls all night long.

He has even ordered new business cards. Tonight, he hands me one of his cards, which reads:

## JACE ALLMAN

*Why fish from water,*
*when you can fish from sky?*

"Get it?" he whispers.

I do. Owls are predators. That's why he likes to lure them in, despite stories of the woods, old stories of people attacked by owls. I want to tell him these stories, but then I change my mind. I'm afraid for the ambassador owl.

The first time I saw the owl, I felt I had seen something special: a secret friend, a kinship in its gaze, the way I felt the first time I saw Jace.

After downloading a recording on his smartphone, an owl hooting during mating season, Jace sits quietly to wait for dusk on the balcony. Clutching a large flashlight, he pushes play to start the recording. Eventually, the owl answers back. We can hear it far away before it appears. Why, I wonder, is Jace taking such a risk? He's doing it, I think, to please me, but also for the thrill, the challenge. Inventing a new sport. To entertain himself and the neighbors. Because he can't sleep. Perhaps even because he feels guilty that I gave up birding to care for him. And yet, I'm keeping a secret from him. I think what he's doing is wrong and want him to stop. Instead, I tell him it's great and I love it.

I worry. What would really happen if he caught the ambassador owl? Owls are usually secretive and don't like being seen by humans, so why and how would one be willing? Maybe, I suspect, it's because the owl is wounded and must care for its brood in times of rodent shortage.

The owl sits in the oak, staring down at Jace.

"Bait," Jace whispers to me as the owl watches us. Jace looks at the owl as if it might answer. "What do owls like to eat?"

"Rodents," I say.

"A rat or squirrel on a hook and string will chew through or run under the house. That's no good. I need something that will fly."

"Sparrows?" I ask. "Bats?"

"Bats!"

✛ ✛ ✛

In the morning, we're in bed in the dark when Jace rises early. I don't hear him using his ramps and handrails. The room is too dark for me to see what's happening, but his silhouette seems to float from his side of the bed to the bathroom. I blink, attempting to focus. I don't want to startle him like the owls I used to watch. If something is helping him rise above his troubles, I don't want to stop it. I want to help him hold onto the spirit that's lifting him.

When I finally get out of bed and have my coffee, dawn has broken. In the soft morning light, I go out to search for Jace. His empty wheelchair is sitting beside the carport.

"Jace? Jace!" I call.

"Up here," he shouts from the top of the carport. He explains that he's stapling a net over a hole, a gap between the brick wall and the carport's metal roof.

"How did you get up there?" I ask.

"It's the bats' only door. I've seen them flying in and out in the evenings," Jace says with a twisted smile.

"But how? How did you see them flying out up there?"

"I go up here all the time." He laughs.

I wonder where he really goes when he ventures out to "get fresh air."

"It doesn't seem fair," I say at night when he nets the first bat, brown velvet wings flopping in terror as Jace holds it writhing in his heavy leather gloves. Now we're both ignoring that he's doing the impossible, being up on the carport roof yet again. What is he up to in the dark?

Sitting on top of the carport, Jace grabs his rod and reel, then ties twine to the foot of the thrashing, squealing bat.

"How did you get your fishing gear up there?" I ask.

He attaches the twine to fishing line on the rod and reel, so the bat is connected. He says, "Wait and see. I'll just test it tonight. I'll not call the owl yet."

The bat begins to fly, connected to the fishing line. Jace gives it more line, letting it out farther and higher. "Look at it go," he says with a smile.

He carefully reels the bat back in, grabs it in his gloved hands, and cuts it free from the twine and line. Released and free, the bat flies away, disappearing into the darkening sky above the trees.

"Well?" I ask, thinking what Jace is proposing to do to the owl will require great skill, unlike what he has just done to the bat.

"Before I start fishing for owls, I need to fish for more bats."

He fishes for bats by threading a large moth on line and flying it outside the bat hole. A bait bat is finally caught, mouth tangled in the line while devouring the moth. Jace secures the bat, throwing a net over it, then knotting twine threaded with fishing line on its leg. Now, he's playing a recording of owl mating calls. When the ambassador owl answers, flying toward him, Jace lets the bait bat fly on the line to lure the owl. Jace fishes with the bat, live bait flying through the dark sky on line, attached to rod and reel.

Jace almost gets the owl, but not quite, giving up, waiting for another night. Only for a few minutes, I go inside the house to start the coffee. When I got back outside, Jace is down from the carport and sitting in his wheelchair.

"Is everything alright?" I ask, not wanting to let him know how suspicious I'm becoming. Perhaps he doesn't realize. I worry calling attention to the impossible could stop it from happening again.

To keep the owl interested, Jace uses sounds I collected long ago on old tapes from a recorder placed near a nest box outside my childhood bedroom window, when I spent nights listening to owls' whistles, cackles, grunts, and growls. Jace begins to mimic these sounds. He hoots at dusk, pulls out his smartphone, finds the birdcall app, and plays the owls' mating call. Then, he cranks up the old tape player on max volume, hooking it up to speakers to play the sounds I recorded long ago.

The ambassador owl flies nearer.

I perch on the back porch beneath the balcony. Under the plastic awning faded from sun, I sip a mojito with muddled mint from our garden. I'm watching Jace on the balcony near the treetops while pretending to watch the owl.

Jace catches the ambassador owl as it swoops in for the bait bat. I hear screams and laughter, whispers. He reels the owl on strong line, netting it with the bat in its beak.

Jace deposits the stunned owl in one of the tree cages connected to pulleys. He uses his system of boxes and lines and pulleys to bring fresh cages to the balcony and then to return them to the trees, where they dangle like rustic chandeliers from oak limbs. A struggle even for him, Jace captures the mate of the caged owl next.

The stunned owls reanimate in cages. They stir, dazed, coming to inside chandeliers lit by solar landscape spotlights. After drawing them nearer with the pulley, Jace opens the cage doors with a long-clawed pointer, much larger than the one he uses to reach the newspaper on the driveway.

The owls fly free.

The neighbors applaud. Jace motions for silence, and they obey his unspoken command.

On the balcony under the pecan trees, he calls to the owls, again, getting them to call back. It scares me the way they stare as they answer back, as if trying to hold a conversation with Jace. He's setting up his laptop with more owl recordings on the balcony table under the pecan trees. These are not mating calls but the calls of young owls, nestlings, calling to their parents. I fear he will anger the owls and we'll pay the price of his foolish game.

Over the course of many nights, Jace and the owls have conversations. Now that he has learned to lure them, to mimic their voices, they answer. In the pecan trees near the balcony, the owls roost, calling to him even as he lures them nearer.

The calls become louder, increasing in intensity, and then I hear another sound, unlike any that I have heard before when Jace fishes for owls. His voice changes and is not at all owl-like but the screech of a little boy, frightened, overwhelmed. When I hear his little-boy cry, my maternal instincts kick in, and I rush up the rickety rails leading from the porch to the balcony, where I find he has netted a great horned owl so large it won't fit inside the cages. Jace doesn't know what to do now that he's got it.

"Let him go," I say.

Jace says, "Out of the way!"

Jace is trying to cut it loose, but the owl is staring up at the inky sky, taking off too fast, beating its wings, slapping Jace's face. Jace's nose is bleeding; he holds onto his fishing pole. It whips crazily in his large hands as the owl circles above. Jace reels the owl in as it swerves higher, pulling away. He's giving it more line, and yet the line threatens to wrap around the branches of the nearer trees.

"I'll wear him down," he says.

God knows if he'll be able, or what he'll do with the owl if he succeeds.

The owl wants to escape with the bait. It weaves above, circling down. Jace reeling, reeling, huffs out of breath. Sweating profusely, he attempts to pull the owl from the sky. The line breaks. Jace falls back against his wheelchair, the pole still in his hands, the great horned owl disappearing into the dark.

"One thing I'll never buy again," he says, catching his breath, "is cheap line."

Something about the wild look in his eye makes me remember the way we used to love each other. I don't want him fishing for owls anymore because he might get hurt or hurt one of the owls and be sorry.

✢ ✢ ✢

By next evening, Jace switches to sparrows while searching for more bats and flying squirrels.

Past midnight, he's toying with the new line and the sparrows in their cages.

"When I was a kid," I say, "a man named Jimmy got too close to a great horned owl during mating season. Its talons clamped through his skull like an industrial claw tearing through old metal."

"No kidding?" asks Jace.

"Jimmy had a lobotomy — a lobotomy by owl."

Jace gazes up to the darkening sky as if thinking about owls in a new way. He wheels back inside the house, without fishing for owls tonight. I hope I've convinced him to see reason, but in the morning, he's in the garage with his welder, working on something that resembles a medieval torture device.

"What's that for?" I ask.

Jace doesn't answer, and I fear for the owls.

When I was a child, my grandpa told me that young barn owls can be generous toward each other, donating portions of their food to smaller, hungrier siblings. My family had too many children and step-children left at our door, cousins and second cousins, friends of in-laws. With so many in the house to properly feed and care for, we needed an altruism rare among animals to survive.

With the younger children, I learned to communicate wordlessly. Before dropping out of high school, I was listening to owls in the nest box outside my window. Owls I associated with Athena's shining eyes. The children cried out in trills, barks, and hoots at night, answering the owls.

We can be generous to each other, I think. We can be generous to each other, like owls.

Tonight, Jace resembles an owl when he gazes at me in moonlight, his pale face flat and heart-shaped like a barn owl's facial disk that functions as a kind of satellite to capture sound. I never tell Jace about my childhood. He wouldn't understand, just as he wouldn't appreciate how I love the owls for their calls and their silence, the way their feathers have serrated fringes that reduce noise in flight as velvety wings absorb sound. Jace would never understand how what he's doing could alert predators to the owls' whereabouts, make the owls worry for their young, give a lonely owl false hope of finding a mate, or even lure fledglings from the nest.

I committed that crime against nature more than once, and I paid the price as a young girl. After nights of luring owls, I was lured by a false mating call from a married man I thought loved me before leaving me forever damaged. I want to tell Jace. Instead, I tell him owls vocalize differently in spring, when looking for a mate than they do in early summer, when defending their young. This gives him an idea. He uses his laptop and smartphone to listen to more recorded owl calls captured in the wild.

"Thanks, babe," Jace says.

I want to tell him about what happened to me, how a mating call can be used against a lonely girl, a lonely boy, an isolated woman or a defeated man. He only thinks of protecting his head from talons. That's why he goes into the garage to collect metal rods and to fire up his old welder again.

I sip my mojito and look away from the torch light.

When he's finished welding, he holds up a metal contraption, a cage for a man's head.

Sure enough, he puts it on, his eyes staring out of the bars.

"Jace," I say.

"Baby," he says. "How about a kiss?"

He puckers up and makes kissing sounds inside the cage.

Laughing, I go back inside the house. I'm afraid to look out the window when I hear the jigsaw. He's making screw boards for his arms.

"What now?" I whisper.

His arms are braced by boards locked into place by screws. Hinged at the elbow, the boards open at his hands so he can manipulate the fishing pole and pulleys.

The next day, Jace sets up the laptop as the sun goes down over the trees, the sky whitening with that faint graying just before it darkens. Before picking up his rod and reel, Jace puts on his gear and begins to play the recording to lure the great horned owl. I see it landing on the branches.

Jace reaches inside the sparrow cage to remove the first one tied to bait the line. Slowly, he releases the sparrow so that it flies into the sky, one foot hooked. Jace gives it some slack before flying it closer to the owl. This owl is the big one, large enough to kill a man. Every time Jace gets the great horned owl on the line, circling above, and then cuts the line to let it go, I realize he's afraid.

Watching from the other side of the kitchen window, I hold my breath. My heart skips. The great horned owl, now caught on the line again, swoops down to land on the board attached to Jace's left arm. Jace cuts the line, but the owl stays put, holding the sparrow in its beak while staring into Jace's cage.

When the owl finally flies away with the sparrow, Jace rolls back into the house. He makes love to me like he hasn't since before he lost his legs.

"Catch and release," he says, smiling.

The next night, like every other night, Jace wheels out onto the balcony and puts the cage on his head and the boards on his arms. I watch from the window, and the neighbors watch from the other side of the fence, taking videos on smartphones.

Jace plays the recording of the great horned owl, luring it to the yard.

For the rest of that year and into the next, the big owl keeps coming back, getting used to Jace and taking one bait after another to the trees. Jace keeps feeding the big owl. It lands on him one night and doesn't let go. Rising toward the moon, Jace and the owl fly, the pecan trees below.

# The Mushroom Suit

When my young husband died unexpectedly, I wanted to find the
perfect coffin for an open casket. He was so tall it would have to be
custom-made. I couldn't imagine it any other way. I wanted to see David
again at his funeral. I knew his eyes would be closed. I would never see
his eyes again, but I could see his peaceful face at rest, as if sleeping, his
square dimpled chin smooth and freshly shaven. His lips slightly smiling
as if he had kept a secret from us all, he would be meticulously dressed
in an elegant suit with a dapper salmon silk tie. His golden curls always
smelled of evergreens. I wanted to lean down, to kiss his forehead and
smell his hair once more. To mourn him, to honor him, I wanted closure.
I imagined how his mother and his father would feel, seeing David laid
to rest in the best coffin money could build.

I assumed an old-fashioned funeral would be healing. One day,
I expected, we would visit David's exquisitely landscaped gravesite,
marked with a large marble headstone and a magnificent imposing
statue in the local cemetery with its painted iron gates opening off
the highway.

These thoughts soothed me — the gravesite, the statue, the
headstone, the coffin, David's body pristinely displayed in the church
for gathering mourners. Even so, I couldn't settle with the knowledge
of how we lost him. None of us had been ready. It was a terrible shock.
So terrible it didn't seem real.

That's why I started laughing when I found his body.

Certain people, especially his parents, have a hard time forgiving
me for that.

Faking his death was a game David played with me. Each time,
he would gaze at me, strangely, studying my reaction. He would laugh

and put on the weird cream-colored pajama with a full mask that buttoned over his face. The pajama had gloves and slippers, so none of him was uncovered, no skin exposed. No holes for eyes, it troubled me, worse than the bogus deaths he put me through. Something about the weird pajama broke me. It was impossible to have sex or cuddle when he wore it to bed. It was as if he were shutting me off, shutting me out. Inside that pajama, he was hidden, repeatedly.

"What have you done?" I asked when I found him in the living room. Slumped on the sofa, he was dressed for work in a gray suit. I thought he was playing games, but I was shocked to see the suit was ruined. "David? What's this?"

Blood, lots of blood, dripped, splashed. On the ceiling. On the stereo. On the television. On the mantel. On the sofa. On the curtains. On the windows. On the walls. Hair hung in blood. The back of his head, wet and messy; splatter covered his face. A gun cradled in his right hand, a bullet lodged in drywall.

I was furious, thinking how difficult it would be to wipe the syrupy stuff off the ceiling and wash it out of the sofa and curtains.

I shook him. He was limp. Unresponsive. This was another of David's tricks, I thought. He was a decent actor. He did things like this, using fake blood to scare me. All the time, pretending to be limp, dead.

He wasn't acting. He was gone.

Just like that, I found the weird pajama laid out in another room, on our bed.

"I would have appreciated a trigger warning," I said, though he couldn't hear me.

That's when his older sister Melanie arrived, before I had the chance to dial 911. A Realtor who worked with David, she was tall like him, statuesque and daunting. Dressed for a closing in a tailored charcoal pantsuit, she wore cinnamon lipstick matching her high heels.

"Don't come in here," I said.

"Why?" Melanie asked, opening the screen door and pushing past me with her designer shoes clacking on the tile. "Where's David? Why wasn't he at the closing?"

She strutted into the living room to stop short in front of David on the sofa. I realized I was witnessing the moment her life was changing.

She looked at me as if I were a murderer.

I laughed.

She fell on the rug. Weeping, her nose rested between David's large, polished dress shoes.

I laughed for hours. I laughed when the police arrived. I laughed at the ambulance. I laughed at the coroner. No one was laughing with me. They looked at me with pity. When his parents found me laughing at the police station, they told me to go to hell, where I belonged. But in my mind, hell was where David was. It was where he had gone. I didn't know how to tell them. According to my religion, I had lost him forever because of his suicide, which meant no heaven for him. His family refused to believe he killed himself. They blamed me. Literally. They told the police I should be investigated for murder. The police just gazed at me as if they couldn't believe what I was doing. I laughed, until I wanted to cry but couldn't.

I answered all their questions, several times, still laughing. Always laughing.

They started to smile at me.

In hindsight, I can see I married a suicidal male. David knew it all along, what he would do. He knew what he was going to do long before he met me. He tried to warn me. He told me I should marry someone else, someone who would stick around. I was worried he would leave me. I just didn't know where he was going.

After the police told me I was free to leave the interview room, after hours and hours of talking at the station, they told me I had to be escorted home.

My in-laws showed up to drive me to their home, since they said that I shouldn't be at my home, until we could hire professional cleaners. I was still laughing, and it was starting to hurt because I couldn't stop.

"Alright, alright," David's father said. David's gracefully uptight mother was so furious, she wouldn't even look at me. Unlike David, his father was short and squat. David's mother was the tall parent, but her personality remained humorless, not at all like David, the practical joker.

"Calm down. Settle down, Gillian," said David's father, staring at me with something like pity as he opened the car door. I climbed into the back of the Lexus. It still smelled new, as if David's parents had been taking it for an extended test drive. "You okay, dear?" David's father whispered as David's mother got into the front seat, passenger side. David's father closed the door and stared through the windows. I realized he was beginning to think I was so overwhelmed with grief that I was caught in the grip of hysteria. Was I? "You're not right, are you, girl?" he asked, just before he started the Lexus, as if there were something truly wrong with me. As he drove down dark streets with me laughing quietly and David's mother sitting stiffly in her straitjacket of silence, streetlights appeared haloed in rainbows, blurry out the Lexus windows.

Just when I was about to stop laughing inside their tastefully decorated house with its view of the country club's ninth hole, David's parents kept saying funny things to make me laugh. I wondered if they had sex in their hot tub, like David and I had done when they were away. I kept imagining David's parents having sex as they said absurd, ridiculous things about David and their plans for his funeral. I wondered if they were just like David, after all, because the bizarre things they were saying were just the type of things he might have said, to get a rise out of me at the most inappropriate moment.

"We want him buried in a mushroom suit," his father said.

"A what?" I asked, not believing my ears. "Because of the incident at Mellow Mushroom, with the mushroom pizza? My god, did David finally tell you about that? Unbelievable. I thought he'd never admit it. I thought he'd die first," I said, recalling the notorious incident that got us kicked out of the restaurant, where we were waiting for our mushroom pizza.

"What incident?" his mother asked.

Bless their hearts, I thought, they're trying to help me, to make me feel better. To humor them, because they were humoring me, I explained what happened at the Mellow Mushroom, when the manager threatened to call the cops on David.

David was drawing a mushroom on a napkin when a horde of elementary-school children arrived by the busload and began loitering beside our table, getting rowdy. To entertain them, David showed them the mushroom drawing. The next thing I knew, the kids' teacher approached to say David was a disgusting man and should be ashamed of himself. She called him a pedophile. We thought she had confused him with another man. I tried to tell her she had the wrong person. The manager then approached our table and asked us to leave.

"Why?" David asked. "What did we do?"

"That," said the manager. "That. Look at that! What is that? You can't have that in here."

"What?" I asked, staring down at David's drawing. "This?"

"Oh, god," whispered David, under this breath.

"It's illegal to show that to children," said the manager. "I could call the cops. Now, scram!"

David and I gazed down at the drawing on his napkin and realized his drawing resembled a mushroom-headed dick. The restaurant manager, the teacher, and the children all thought my husband was drawing a dick on a napkin to show to children. David and I tried to explain it was a misunderstanding. Examining the drawing in a new light, I realized the manager would never believe us. David's friends entered the restaurant, just in time to follow us into the parking lot, asking what happened. They began teasing David mercilessly for his drawing. Not knowing what to do, I gave the drawing to David's friends, who thanked me profusely and had it framed.

"He told you about that?" I asked David's parents. I covered my mouth with my hands and burst out laughing, hard. I snorted. I imagined David dressed as a giant mushroom. David in a mushroom costume! David! David dressed as a mushroom for his own funeral. God, he would have loved that.

Then, because of the look on his parents' faces, I wondered if someone had given me something other than a sedative.

Maybe I misheard? No, they assured me I had heard correctly. David's family wanted him buried in a mushroom costume. That, I thought, was funny. Hysterical. A great joke. I congratulated his mother on her sense of humor. I couldn't stop laughing. "Oh, god," I said. "A mushroom costume. Oh, lord. That's rich."

His mother just stared at me, and I realized she was dead serious as she explained the suit wasn't a mushroom costume. Made of mushrooms and organic cotton and seeded with mushroom spores, it decomposed a human body while cleaning toxins before they reached the soil. She said, "We're all full of toxins, you and me and David. Most people carry BPA, heavy metals, preservatives, even pesticides. We also carry nutrients."

"I can't deal with this," I said.

"Mushrooms are nature's cleaners. Even edible varieties are great at cleaning soil," said David's father. "David's suit has spores from edible varieties but also from a customized hybrid mushroom bred to decompose David's flesh."

"How can that be?" I asked, feeling sick.

"It's like pajamas covered in netting full of spores," said his father.

"No," I said, sinking at the mention of the word pajamas. I started to remember the weird pajamas David wore the year before he died. Were those weird pajamas a burial shroud?

"You just said you would be fine with him dressed in a mushroom costume at his funeral! Now, you're saying you won't allow him to be buried in a mushroom suit?" his mother asked.

As she poured our coffee, I realized she wanted to deny me a classic coffin for the classically handsome, statuesque man she had borne and I had lost. I had never seen a man as healthy or as exquisite as David before and knew I never would again. He was taller than other men and had extremely refined symmetrical features with a friendly smile that opened doors usually closed to others. It was hard to explain that no one who met him or even saw him in passing would have thought he was the sort of man to kill himself.

His mother wanted to allow mushrooms to devour his gorgeous body. She wanted him to be food for mushrooms. I wanted him properly prepared, preserved, embalmed. His father wouldn't hear of it. His mother accused me of wanting to poison the earth with her son's corpse.

"His body, his body," was all I could say between sobs. Choking on the piping hot French roast his mother had poured into an elegant teacup, I shivered, remembering being naked with David, the way he held me as I kissed his face, his neck. I kissed him everywhere he would allow me. Then, I kissed him more.

"Don't you see?" asked his father. "We could all be a part of this, with David forever."

"It's what he wanted," said his mother. "From his body, the mushroom suit will feed a fruit tree, and its fruit will feed our bodies. When we all die, we'll be buried in mushroom suits, like David. The seeds from his tree can be planted in us. When his tree dies and our trees die, others will grow from the seeds in us. We will become seed savers and a family orchard, so none of David ever goes to waste or ever really leaves us. From his body, we will become part of an orchard to feed each other and the world."

"I don't know," I said, feeling nauseated from the coffee on my empty stomach. "It seems untraditional."

"So," said his mother, "you'd rather David's body be pumped full of gallons of toxic embalming fluid to leech out into a casket in a cemetery of pesticides?"

"Yes," I said. "Yes! That's what I want."

His mother gasped. She said his body would be buttoned inside a burial suit seeded with fungus feeding on his flesh. "They'll devour what's left of him," she said. "See, it's beautiful? They'll live on him, long enough to feed something else, which will feed something else, which will one day feed us."

"Why?" I asked. I imagined mushrooms eating his toes, his eyes, every part of him I had kissed and licked and sucked: his tongue, his dick, his balls dangling like delectable plums. I loved him so much that when we were making love I felt as if I could eat him alive. That was why I couldn't bear putting my husband inside a suit lined with flesh-eating mushrooms. What wife could?

"It's simple and practical," his father said. "Don't be a baby, Gillian."

"How? How is it simple?" I asked, thinking a coffin and funeral with an open casket was traditional, dignified, certain.

"Would you really rather him be embalmed, put in a coffin with a concrete liner, and buried in a cemetery?" his father asked.

"Yes," I said. "I would."

"Why do all that harm to the environment? That's not what he wanted," said his father.

But what about what I wanted? Did that matter? Apparently not. I guess I was the selfish one. "But what about his body? He said it was mine," I said.

"What do you mean?" his mother asked.

I told her sex was the one good thing about our marriage. The sex was fabulous, the best either of us ever had and we did it all the time, in every room of our house and theirs. We did it in cars and in bathrooms at parties. We did it outdoors and in public places, often in theaters, amusement parks, churches, buses, pools, and diners, and in the houses and buildings he listed as a Realtor. It healed us and brought us closer. It confirmed and restored our love. I remember touching him, lying beside him, licking him, sucking him, riding him, kissing him all over, the way he kissed me as he buried his exquisite dick deep inside me like a secret between us. I thought we would keep doing it for decades. I thought we would never stop. We gave our bodies to each other, repeatedly. That was why I wanted to be buried beside him, for our bodies to be put to rest the same way, near each other, though now I understood my coffin wouldn't be needed for decades, though he needed his coffin now. His body needed his coffin to hold it for me because I couldn't hold his body anymore.

I was, after all, very acquainted with his body, even if I hadn't known what was in his mind. None of us knew all the things he had been thinking or what he was planning. What happened was a complete shock, at least for me. I've always assumed that's what started all the disagreements about his burial.

"There were so many things you never knew about him," his mother said. "So much he never told you. Things he told his father and me that he could never tell his wife."

"You bitch!" I shouted.

"At least you're not laughing anymore," said his mother, smiling.

"What did he tell you? What did you know about him that I don't know? I slept with him. He put his dick inside me. Doesn't that count for something?" I asked.

"Not in the way you think," his mother said.

I started to cry, finally, and she put her hand on my shoulder and explained he was part of something called the Suburban Death Project.

"David and I took a do-your-own-death workshop for home burial," his mother said. "We did it together. His father is also in on it. We were planning for all our deaths — yours included."

"It soothed David in ways you'll never know, and it's a comfort to us now," said his father.

"It was his passion, his hobby. He could never share it with you, but he shared it with me and his father," said his mother.

"No!" I needed to vomit. My head was spinning.

I longed for a coffin. I needed a coffin. Only a coffin would satisfy my needs to lay David to rest in a style that would allow me to feel I could let go and show my love for him. The thing no one wanted to speak about was how very young he was. And how unexpectedly he died. And how beautiful the corpse. It hurt me. It was a pain like no other. David and I weren't even of legal drinking age yet. I thought we had decades ahead of us.

I felt a familiar taste in my mouth, blooming behind my tongue and through my teeth. It was mushrooms — the earthy flavors of the mushroom dinners David used to prepare for me. I couldn't tell his mother that. I couldn't tell anyone. I couldn't hardly even admit it to myself since I was raised in a conservative religion where despair was the greatest sin. I was raised to believe my young husband had gone to hell for what he had done, and that I would be going to heaven, so his body was all that was left of him, at least for me. I didn't want to give it up to mushrooms.

Mushrooms! For God's sakes! The thought wasn't so much gross as it was indignant. David and I ate mushrooms all the time — on pasta and on pizza and in quiche. It was one of our favorite foods. He was supposed to eat mushrooms, not the other way around. I had lost him, really lost him, and my loss was mushrooms' gain. Now my gorgeous man, who used to eat mushrooms, would be fed to mushrooms. Now that his soul had gone to hell, I couldn't stand to lose his body to something as passive as mushrooms fashioned into a suit to devour the flesh from his bones.

"Think of all the money you'll save on the coffin and on embalming," said David's father. "He's already paid for the suit. He raised the mushrooms with the help of a lab. They were bred just for his body and taught to hunger for him. David trained them and grew them. He cared for his mushrooms."

"We were married. His body is mine!" I said, again, but in saying this I told his mother the wrong thing. She slapped me. Both of us were surprised, not so much by the slap but for the simple fact that it had the ability to surprise us both. We had both lost ourselves in losing David and had been walking in a fog of pain, a stupor of grief, both of us hating each other but vaguely because so much of our energy was focused on fighting over his body while living without him. It had only been one day since he died, and his mother and I had been arguing for hours, sleeping little.

Losing him was like losing myself but that was such a cliché I couldn't even say it to anyone. All I knew was the love of my life, my husband, needed to be buried. Soon.

I told his mother again, because I thought it might comfort his mother to know how much I loved him.

"Suicides, the experts say, increase in May," she said. "Something about the spring, the blossoms and the warm weather. The longer days and the sunlight, the beauty of the robins and the roses. Something about the hope of the new season. No one knows why, dear. David was part of that trend, the May suicides."

I would always hate the month of May after that.

Apparently, David and his mother had plans for his body that didn't include me, among them, a customized burial on his family's acreage.

"David was part of an online group of healthy people who discuss plans for their death," his mother said. "He was extremely active in the group."

"You could have stopped him," I said. "You could have told me." I hated her, more than ever, because I started to wonder why she didn't tell me, why she didn't try to stop him. It was almost as if she had enough information to know what he would do. But did I?

"Don't deny his mushrooms," she said, "the ones he raised and trained to eat him. Don't kill what he worked so hard to keep alive."

I covered my mouth with my hands, retching as I remembered his little project in the basement: the mushroom garden he had been growing. He was very particular, watching them grow, misting them in the shadows and feeding them secretly. Once, I caught him putting hair from his hairbrush and his fingernail clippings into the soil where the mushrooms grew. When he cut his nails, he took to standing over the mushroom garden, letting the toenail clippings fall into the soil near the mushrooms. Whenever he got a haircut, he saved the hair and buried it in the soil of that garden. Feeding the hybrid mushrooms his own hair and nails, he taught them, just like his mother and father had said. David was training the hybrid mushrooms to hunger for him. What made me sick was how often he cooked with the edible varieties — making the two of us intimate, gourmet meals with mushrooms before we made love in the kitchen, on the table and on the tile. He would sometimes gather the mushrooms and seal them into plastic bags in padded envelopes to mail.

To calm myself, I closed my eyes while imagining gorgeous, jewellike caskets, starting with a midnight blue deluxe casket, a deep blue reflecting the midnight sky. My sister had told me to order a black casket with white velour interior from Overnight Caskets, though a funeral director informed me majestic mahogany is for "special loved ones." What about for loved ones who aren't special? I wondered. Then, I glimpsed the orchid steel casket — strong durable steel in antique orchid with a starburst design, so soft. What about the simple pine casket? My mother had asked, informing me I could order it from Amazon. I knew she wanted me to get a cheap coffin because she worried about my finances, and for some reason that hurt like hell. What about the traditional oak? she asked. David wasn't that traditional, I had to remind her.

While a stainless-steel casket is only $2,700, a copper casket is $2,900. But the bronze casket with a white velvet body is $6,900. My favorite was the Xiao En Center Casket with its fine mahogany wood, burgundy velvet interior, and hand-painted artistic accents, but it cost $36,400. My mother said that was obscene.

"Think of what David would have wanted," David's mother said, still arguing. His mother was probably right. But what did it matter? He wasn't here anymore. She was. He probably would have wanted to just disappear into mushrooms, to degrade beneath a tree, coffinless, to just disappear into a suit of mushrooms so that he would become something else, gently but quickly, all evidence of him absorbed into a sack of fugus tailored to devour his remains. His handsome remains. His mother started crying, asking, "Why, why won't you give him what he wanted? This one last thing."

That's when I realized one of us would have to be the one to steal his body from the other. One of us would take his body away from the other. Since I was his wife, there would be no contest. Legally, his body was mine because there had been no formal will. Despite everything, he had left all details up to me. But why, why, his mother kept asking, wouldn't I give David what he would have wanted?

Maybe, I began to think, just maybe, he assumed I would give him what he wanted, even if it wasn't what I wanted. Maybe, just maybe, he didn't really want what he claimed he wanted. Just like maybe, just maybe, he didn't really want to die. There were days he wanted to live, and there were days he knew he would kill himself and wanted someone to stop him.

Was it possible that all of this — the mushroom suit, the mushroom garden, the gourmet mushroom meals, the mushroom-headed dick on a napkin — might have been some sort of an elaborate cry for help I was unable to answer?

I didn't know.

His mother kept asking me why I wouldn't just give David what he wanted.

I didn't answer his mother's question, though the answer was clear and simple. It was something his mother could never understand. Why wouldn't I give him what he wanted? Because what he wanted was to destroy himself. That's what he wanted all along. By loving him so intensely and by giving him all I had to give, I tried to keep him from doing it for as long as I possibly could. Because I loved him, I didn't want him to have what he wanted, even in death. And now, once again, I was going to have to let him have what he wanted because he was never really mine.

Over the years, everything changed among us because of what I allowed David's parents to do with David's body. I caved. I let David be buried in the mushroom suit, and everything was nothing like I thought it would be. There was no open casket, no casket, no viewing, no headstone, no statue.

Instead, there was a peach tree.

David's parents allowed me to select a young peach tree from a tree farm in Georgia. The tree was supposed to produce large, sweet fruit. His father carefully placed the peach tree in the soil over David's body after installing an incubator with a sensor embedded in the soil. The sensor sent custom updates, going right to our smart phones through an app that monitored the health of the growing peach tree. It grew from David's body, wrapped in the mushroom suit, which became a biodegradable urn.

Our modest family goal was to be able to eat David's peaches in three years' time.

"I hope the mushrooms start to eat him faster," said his mother, checking the tree on the app. She had so many plans for the peaches — fresh peach pie, peach fritters, peach ice cream, peaches and cream, peach cobbler, peach bread, canned peaches, and peach preserves.

Me? I just wanted to pick a single perfect peach and eat it straight from the tree. That was all.

For David's family and for me, eating the peaches that grew from his tree would connect us to him, nourishing us. Eating the fruit that grew from the nutrients of his decomposed body would be the closest we ever came to sharing life after death. Planning the moment of eating the peaches felt both strange and sacred.

When the peaches were finally ready for us to harvest, they had grown round and bright with yellow and pink skin, like the warm colors braided into the sky at sundown.

The peaches tasted like the sweetness of our love mingling with a strong tartness making my tongue ache, reminding me of how David loved me and how he hurt me. How it hurt to love him and to lose him. Biting into the first peach, I tasted his sadness and his love.

# What Goes on Near the Water

My mother and I walk through a grove of Canadian Hemlock after
the rain. I'm three and collecting small egg-shaped cones. I rub their
smooth light brown scales against my palms. Tree hugger, I run from
tree to tree and embrace the conifers along the woodland brooks,
nearing the gingerbread-style Victorian, where more hemlocks stand
a few feet apart, forming a privacy hedge. I must be wandering from
her, toward the house, because she calls after me afraid of what I don't
understand. "Don't go there!" she cries. "Don't go that way! Come back
to me!" I run to her, away from the house and through the pyramid-
shaped trees, past their graceful lacey leaves and tapering trunks. I
run to the hemlock's edge, where she's waiting. She's holding out her
arms to embrace me. "Here, Laney, here," she whispers. "Stay with me,"
lifting me into her arms, holding me close, "Safe." We hug; she smells
like hemlock.

I never see her again. I see her again. I don't know. It's the last
time I see her or very near the last. I don't know. I'm too young.

Now, I'm an adult, a decade older than my mother the last time I saw
her, and my biggest regret is not remembering her face. I close my
eyes to see her, but her face is gone, and my grandparents don't have
any photographs of her. They say they don't have photographs of my
father, either. They didn't know him well. He left too soon. But what
about my mother? They won't tell me. And I stop asking. Questions
upset Grandmother.

I have no memory of my father. His face, his voice, nothing.

Time attacks memory the way old hemlocks are attacked by woolly adelgid.

✢ ✢ ✢

I remember it happening the summer before I turned seventeen. I can still see Grandfather spraying chemicals on the hedge as our privacy falls away, exposing the old gingerbread Victorian we live in, just the three of us. The hemlock hides the house from the road. Woolly adelgid attacks the hemlocks, and there's nothing Grandfather can do to stop it.

I think back to a time when the sea moves me. I'm sixteen, mesmerized by expansive gray waters changing colors with the sunset and the dawn. On that day, a houseboat putters along the edge of the water before the small-boat races entertain camper sailors who pitch tents on either side of lock. Tommy lives there, but Grandfather has forbidden me to go, because of the "drifters" and "grifters," because of "what goes on near the water."

Once a professional diver and an underwater welder, Grandfather was gone for months at a time before his retirement, working for the oil companies. Grandmother, a retired family-law attorney, stays inside the house making candles, sipping coffee, and doing yoga in rooms decorated with inherited macramé and Polish pottery.

Walking inside the living room, I find her tending the wispy green hanging plants, mostly ferns. "Do you remember what we said about curfew?" she asks when I catch her staring out the windows.

"Yeah?" I ask. "Why?"

"Beware of pretty boys," Grandmother says.

Has she seen Tommy sneaking through the hemlock to find me?

"Beauty doesn't last long or lead to any good. Besides, pretty is as pretty — " says Grandmother.

"Whatever," I say.

Curfew talk — our old song and dance. I'm ready to leave. I've finally found someone I want to start a new life with, but Grandmother would never let me go. She lost my mother and doesn't want to lose me, too. But it has been too long, far too long and too lonely here with my questions. I was only three when my grandparents became my parents. My grandparents are not that much older than my classmates' parents. My grandparents give me everything I ever need or want. Except the truth. I ask questions, forbidden questions, questions I know better than to ask again. Why are they raising me? Where have my mother and father gone? Who was my father? Why doesn't my mother come back home, to her own family? Where is she?

The gingerbread Victorian was built to weather snowy days, but on a muggy summer afternoon, the painted walls sweat. The windows are open, letting a warm breeze into all the rooms, except the cool temperature-controlled wine cellar tucked into the farthest corner of the basement. My grandparents hate air-conditioning, but they use it in that one room, where greenish bottles gleam.

When the sun goes down, they retreat into the wine cellar

without me. I hear their laughter through the vents. I hear the pop of corks, the clink of delicate glasses, signaling another private party without me, giving me the perfect opportunity to escape with Tommy. My grandparents stay up late with their wine and then collapse together, happily drunken, only to awaken late and to assume I have gone swimming with other girls.

Tommy holds me gently and takes me with him every night on the sea, where we cuddle on his boat on the dark water. I want him to take his clothes off and swim naked, but he's shy. I want to make love to him. I want him to stay my secret, so Grandmother doesn't suspect him of encroaching upon the cherished hemlocks. Save Tommy, I have few friends, and I think I love him. An expert angler, he lives on what he catches. I like his reels and lures, the way he casts his nets. He fishes for black fish, blue fish, scup, flounder, cod, mackerel, weakfish, ocean catfish, smelt, and shark. After midnight, he anchors with me. In the fogbound morning, we wake to a fish fry or a fish boil with the people who camp along the shore.

That night I watch light move over gentle waves while Tommy swims where low tide bares the pilings of the docks. Fully clothed, he dives deep, treading where the distant lights of summer cottages glow. The summer people will never guess where we go at night, and they will never know how the fog in winter settles over spruce and wild cranberries. Tommy's boat is anchored in eighteen feet of water on a rocky bottom. I watch the shadow move in the lighthouse window and

Tommy ties his boat to a mooring buoy and convinces me to search for the girl in the lighthouse.

I'm afraid to find her, but I don't say why. I'm lucky to have a view of the lighthouse outside my bedroom window. When I was a child, I stared at it every night. Ever since I was just a little girl, when I woke in the morning, I saw it emerge from the mist over the water. The lighthouse meant home to me, the great stone lighthouse that's been sending out its golden beam over the waters since 1892, guiding merchants to the old shipbuilding port, now a playground for the rich. On a clear night, the light can be seen twelve miles away.

Tommy insists there's a homeless runaway living in the lighthouse and then the view from my window is never the same. Who called her Lighthouse Girl first? I imagine her looking out, seeing me seeing her, watching me looking for her.

The raw coast Tommy and I love most has no harbors. We sail ashore to camp near wildflowers and seabirds sleeping. Some nights, we sleep on wildflowers scenting tattered blankets, the soft shawls taken from his boat after he tosses nets onto the water dragging.

What his nets capture: plastic bottles, weeds like hair, eels, blue fish, long, silver fish shining in moonlight, and a woman's gown, shredded and bleached pink like sundown. On the gown, slashes gape near a bloodstain.

The gown looks expensive. There's a rich side and a poor side to these waters. On one shore, the rich own private art galleries and clubs with lighted tennis courts in gated neighborhoods. On the other side, people camp in makeshift tent communities. My grandparents' house sits between the rich side and the poor side. The lighthouse is at the center of it all.

A school of fish surfaces, jumping high as Tommy steers his boat toward a mansion with a pavilion over the water, a place where musicians play. His long hair whips in the wind as he unleashes the sail. A trespasser, Tommy owns the night, and this is more than the rich people in mansions overlooking these waters will ever have. If he were a girl, he would be the best-looking girl in school.

In his boat that night, Tommy tells me a terrible story. I listen carefully, focusing on every detail and getting closer to him, as close as I can get without touching. He's handsome the way some teenage boys are, his skin still soft and smooth, his face frozen on the edge of manhood. I realize why I love kissing him. He's what Grandmother called him: beautiful.

I think he's my age, but I can't tell, and he never answers the same way when I ask how old he is, where his parents are, where his family is living, why he is so alone, and where he comes from. He doesn't like to talk about himself, and this makes me love him more. "I'm Tommy Goggins," he says. "That's all you need to know. I'm Tommy Goggins, and I love you." He's slight and hasn't gotten a beard yet. I love stroking his smooth face when we kiss, but he's shy and won't kiss much or long. His lips are soft. I want to kiss him, but he pushes me away. He's always looking for excuses to avoid getting too physically close. I've never known anyone as modest as he. This makes me want him more. He won't get naked with me, and he wants me to keep my clothes on, even when swimming. I suppose I love Tommy and maybe he loves me, but the only thing he wants to talk about when he holds me on his boat is Lighthouse Girl. Sometimes, I'm afraid he loves her. At first, I thought he was only telling tales to get me to stop kissing him beneath the fog and the blankets covering us on the boat. Now, as the boat drifts closer to the old lighthouse, I think he's invented her to scare me, to keep me from cuddling closer to him. I don't dare confess I began seeing her silhouette.

Each night before I sneak away to be with Tommy, I spy the lighthouse from my bedroom window and the little boat lights twinkling on the black water. Some nights, the mist turns to fog lingering like lace over the waves. An invitation, the night softly veiled and waiting.

No one understands Tommy, what he's doing at night on the boat. I shiver when he asks me to braid his long dark hair.

I don't like to think about what he says, don't believe when he says the girl in the lighthouse ran away from home and is hiding in the lighthouse. The things her family did to her are so horrific she's afraid to speak to anyone or to come out of hiding. In case they might find her and take her back home again. "When she's not in the lighthouse, she's inside the tunnels of the cave," he says. I know the cave he's talking about. It's the cave we often swim toward, where rumored tunnels stretch under the pavilion of the old mansions.

"Want a tour?" Tommy asks, pointing at the cave.

It's dark. He ties his boat to a private dock and cuts off the engine and the lights. We shouldn't be doing what we're doing, but I do it anyway. Trespassers, we leap from the boat to the dock, darting toward the pavilion, Tommy holding my hand, pulling me along, pulling me to jump into the dark waters.

And then we're swimming in our clothes and shoes.

How can I refuse him? Light sparkles on the black water and in his eyes as we swim toward the cliff beneath the mansions' pavilion to the entrance of the cave. He says the rich use hidden tunnels to travel from gallery to gallery, from mansion to mansion. I have never been. Tommy says he has.

"Lighthouse Girl swims into the cave," he whispers, "and walks the tunnels at night."

Swimming with Tommy, I shiver. Two gray whales surface in the distance. The girl is an owl soaring from hemlock to hemlock. Some nights. Other nights, she's a cat hanging on a tree. I don't want to surprise her but I find it hard to stay away.

I don't want to scare her or to catch her like a fish in a net. Watching for her, waiting for her, is like waiting for whales to surface from the waters, like grace. I've felt her presence often, and yet have only seen shadows I've perhaps mistaken for her. Sensing Lighthouse Girl is something like faith, I suspect she's more mythical creature than girl.

Arriving at the cave, we find a rock to hold onto, so we can stop swimming for a while and rest, to catch our breath.

Tommy holds my hand in his, but our grasps keep slipping, and I'm afraid he's letting go.

"What happened to her? What really happened?" I ask Tommy, demanding to know.

He answers and I'm sad, the mystery slipping away, the need to find her, though, only growing.

We let go of the rocks and start swimming, again. The cave is near now, and it only takes a few minutes of swimming before we're crawling toward the rocky entrance, clawing and scraping our way up the jagged edge of the cliff.

Finally, we're inside the cave, but it's so dark and I'm frightened but Tommy pulls me deeper.

A beam of light from the lighthouse moves across the water inside the cave, where our wet shoes slosh through the wake. Tommy's whispering something and I imagine Lighthouse Girl as he described her, what I wanted to know but didn't want to hear: filthy, pregnant, tied up in the dark or chained to a pipe or locked in a closet, hidden away, imprisoned as punishment for getting into trouble, starved, beaten, forgotten. Tommy says the girl broke her chain after the baby was born, and this is how she becomes Lighthouse Girl. I keep thinking I see her everywhere we go at night.

What would it be like to find her or to be found by her? Deep inside the cave, a hollow in the tunnel is shaped like the mouth of a giant fish open to catch water. Tommy and I crawl inside the damp dark tunnel littered with fish bones and eroded stone. I want to ask him why we're searching for her. I want to ask him why he keeps telling me about her. What is she to him? The last ray of light is snuffed out, and I feel him moving closer to me in the dark, but I can't see him anymore. I reach out to touch his body and it doesn't feel the way I thought it would feel and suddenly I know: I have found her.

✣ ✣ ✣

In one version of this story, she is my mother who has been hiding in plain sight, watching over me in terror all during my childhood when I thought I was growing up without her. She was always there, in the lighthouse I watched from my bedroom window.

In another version of this story, the Lighthouse Girl is Tommy. Or rather, Tommy is her. There is no Tommy, or there is no her because she has made herself into Tommy to be near me, to make love to me, to become the boy I need her to be. He is kissing me, as the girl hidden inside him fades away with each kiss. I'm terrified because his mouth is not his mouth.

She is my friend, and she is a girl from school who is invisible to me, who went away, who watched me from a distance. She was lonely like me and needed love like I needed it. Though it tastes like Tommy's mouth, I know it's hers. She whispers to me that she's afraid, that she needs me to go with her deeper inside the cave, and now I am afraid, too. I am also afraid to leave her because I sense she needs me, and we are touching each other, and it feels good. She is naked and undressing me and kissing me. Deeper, deeper, deeper, we go into the darkness of the tunnels.

In the third and final version of this story, she is my mother and she is Tommy. What happens in the cave changes me forever. I go in one person and come out another. I still don't understand what happens in the dark near a sound like wrens trilling, echoing in the tunnels where I first hear her voice. She's just right there with me with the faraway sound of a powerboat cutting the distant wake. I feel her beside me, where Tommy had been, and at first, I think Tommy is gone, just gone. "Tommy?" I whisper. "Tommy, where are you?" I keep calling him, the girl's voice whispering softly in my ear. I'm trying to push her away, but she keeps getting closer, until her lips are pressed to my ear, tickling me the way Tommy always does when he whispers to me. She's speaking so fast in such soft tones I can't understand what she's saying. I realize she's naked beside me, shivering against me, clutching me. I feel her soft, smooth, wet skin, her small breasts trembling like the water. She moves my hands to her breasts and holds them there. I don't know why I know why.

# The Shadow Family

Just as rivers slowly carved valleys into hills, her family's hunger
changed reality. Child of rivers, oceans, and plains, she became a
hidden woman caught between mountains. A girl whose ancestors
grew tomatoes, beans, marijuana, and poppies, she was raven-haired
and sleek with large dark eyes. Like her ancestors' dreams, her life
was nestled between the Pacific Ocean and the foothills of the Sierra
Madre Occidental Range.

At beauty contests, her gaze burrowed into the eyes of strangers
who offered wealth beyond her mother's wildest hopes. A pageant
winner, Elena attracted old men who had somehow managed to
survive as drug traffickers while so many in the cartel had died young.
Guns filled the night with explosions. Hector, the elderly man who
courted her, had more weapons than the police, than the military.
Under gowns, her long, slender body was covered with Hector's hard
kisses, like bruises. Depending on his mood, his kisses were like rain
in the mountains, sun on the plains, or wind across the oceans.

Elena was accustomed to summer rains and subtropical
temperatures of the plains, the moderate warmth of the coast and
valleys. Yet, the weather was cold on Hector's mountain. She wasn't
used to the cold. It was a strange sensation. The chill of the air she
noticed first, the way her flesh shivered in the breeze.

In the mansion full of guns, when Hector first reached out
to Elena, gently encircling her breasts, she discovered what many
pageant winners learned but few lived to tell: the only romance for
captured women is escape. To those who knew her before she held
the title of Miss Sinaloa, she became untouchable.

At night, she dreamed of the mausoleums where traffickers

were buried — Culiacan at sunset, domed buildings silhouetted against blazing sky, *banda* in the distance. Many times, she visited the infamous cemetery of Jardines del Humaya. She didn't want to be buried there. When she died, she wanted her body cremated. Her ashes could float over the desert and find a way back to her family.

Hector seemed to love her so much he frightened her into silence. She cried for him because of what he did not see. The skeletal shadow of Santa Muerte flitted across the concrete rooms of his mansion. Hector was his own god, transporting drugs and women, bribing officials, laundering money. He kept the mausoleums full of fresh bodies and renewed mourners.

✝ ✝ ✝

In the mansion's wine cellar, Elena discovered a corpse, partially preserved and dressed in marijuana leaves and white satin. The woman's flesh was gone, yet her skin remained like dried leather over bones. She was surrounded by candles and tequila bottles. Elena assumed the figure was part of a shrine to Santa Muerte, like so many other shrines with painted skeletons she had seen along the highways.

Because images of Santa Muerte showed a skeleton dressed in white satin and a golden crown, she could be mistaken for the Virgin Mary, except that she was a corpse receiving more petitions for revenge than for protection. Yet Elena's most ardent prayer was to receive a blessed death in a state of grace. Because of Santa Muerte, Elena believed those who were kind to others would find peace, no matter how much violence they suffered in their final moments. Santa

Muerte would torture the torturers in death.

Elena fell in love with the skeleton woman in the wine cellar. Until Santa Muerte, Elena was alone. The skeleton woman was the only one in the mansion Elena did not fear. Prayers gave Elena peace as she caressed bones beneath white satin. She stroked the skull. She left offerings of roses, marijuana, cigarettes, fruit, cigars, and tequila. She lit the candles. She embraced Santa Muerte.

In flickering light, Hector caught her. Elena had been praying, kissing the bones of the corpse's hands and feet. She knelt.

"That's my first wife," Hector said, laughing.

Slowly, Elena began to realize there had been other women in the mansion before her. What happened to the second wife, she learned, was worse than what happened to the first.

Elena romanced the Holy Death. She longed to caress Santa Muerte — the true Santa Muerte — to kiss the bones of her hands, to stroke her skull, and to nuzzle her ribs and clutch her femurs. She would adorn the skeleton with pearls and white satin and become her sister, her lover, her child, her servant, and her maid. It was all Elena wanted. There were men who called Santa Muerte la Niña Blanca, Doña Sebastiana, or la Santísima Muerte. To Elena, she became only *love, my love* — the only reason to lead a virtuous life, the lover that awaited her in death.

A year after discovering Hector's first wife, Elena and eleven powerful men were arrested outside of a military checkpoint near Guadalajara for possession of assault rifles and 1.5 million USD, cash.

During the arrest and subsequent investigation, she kept her head down so that her long hair shadowed her still face. A young woman in a group of brazen men, she kept her hands crossed in front of her legs and looked no one in the eye. Later, the US investigators discovered her English was good and realized she could understand what they were saying, though she preferred not to speak. "Where's Hector?" she finally asked. She wanted to see numerous photos of his body and stared at the photos for days.

"What were you doing?" the investigators asked. "What were you doing in the caravan?"

It was hard to explain that women were cargo. Like guns and money, Elena went where men took her.

The instant she was arrested, she knew she would be stabbed, because that was what Hector had promised. The men who followed his orders were still alive, and he had become their hero by dying.

Secret parties went on in the hills. Fiestas were lures. For every wife or girlfriend murdered, dozens of girls competed to take her place. Drug lords combed the villages; black SUVs with tinted windows rumbled over dirt roads. Girls who wouldn't accept the invitations were kidnapped at gunpoint and taken to ranches. The thrill of sex and fear was alive with music.

More mausoleums were built. The cartels rearranged entire cemeteries by building tombs. The white-domed, windowed buildings contained small, elegant stairs leading to air-conditioned rooms where mourners spoke to giant portraits of murdered men. Everywhere were gifts for the dead — toy machine guns, knives, model cars, and bright balloons swaying above cut flowers in tall marble vases.

Gifts not reserved for the dead were given to the poor. In rural communities, the cartel gained respect through charity, and children longed to become drug lords to please their fathers.

Elena shaved her dark hair and hid it beneath a white-blonde wig in the style of Marilyn Monroe. The name she had been born with was shed the way monarch butterflies shed their chrysalis. The shedding of her identity was part of the government's attempt to save her life.

After testifying against the cartel, Elena moved to the US — to Georgia — and found work as a babysitter for a Christian family called the Lyons. Even though US agents assured Elena that she was safe, she dreamed of being kidnapped by masked men who would hold her, mark her, smother her, and display her body, her corpse. The display was both a calling card and an art form, an exact science. Elena thought the men who posed corpses were sculptors creating work for public and private exhibitions. A single dead woman meant many different things to many different people, depending on the way her corpse was displayed. In Georgia, dreaming of her death, she wondered what message her corpse would send to those who might discover it. She prayed the Lyon children would never know.

The Lyon family embraced Elena as one of their own. They felt sorry for her. She was so lovely, yet so lonely and so uncertain of everything. She was grateful for simple meals and the pleasure of swimming with the children in the little backyard pool. She lived in the Lyons' guest room and went to the movies with the children on Fridays and to church with the family on Sundays.

Because the children always wanted stories, Elena tried to tell the Lyon children peaceful bedtime tales, but she couldn't think of any tales with happy endings. She told the children stories about Hector and Santa Muerte. The children loved Elena because of the stories. It was only when she told them about the shadow family that they began having nightmares.

"Tell us about the shadow family, again," the children demanded, though some of them were so frightened they had tears in their eyes.

"But why?" asked Elena. "Why do you always want to hear about them?"

"Because we're afraid of them."

"Why? They didn't do anything wrong. They were the victims. They were only innocents."

Elena recalled studying the morbid portrait of a young mother and two children in the upstairs rooms of the fancy mausoleum. They were the shadow family she never met. Elena knew what happened, but didn't understand how. Masked men had taken the young mother and her children, who were thrown off a bridge before their mother was decapitated. Her head was delivered to Hector in an icebox; the rest of the mother's body was never found. Finally, the mother's head rested with her children's bodies in the tomb.

After those deaths, revenge killings spread like sickness, a contagion moving across the desert like shadow. One killing inspired another. Men harmed their rivals by killing the women they most loved.

In a secret ceremony, twelve years before he met and married Elena, Hector was already an old man, three times his bride's age. After he escaped from prison, she became his lover, though not by choice. The long-stem roses she accepted meant that she would be raped after the wedding. The ceremony prior to the assault was so lavish that other women were jealous.

Salons specialized in nails and eyelashes for *narco* wives like her. The way she looked and everything she wore reflected her husband's status within the cartel. After eyelash implants, her long, false nails were detailed in crystals, tiny jewels, and small oval portraits of saints.

She was never allowed to leave her husband's clan. Although he had many lovers before her and after her, she was not allowed to speak to other men. Men could be shot just for looking at her. Even though she adored her children, she wanted a lover – a real lover, a man her own age who would whisper to her and caress her. She wanted a man to touch her in a loving way, but she became untouchable.

Flowers, especially roses, terrified her. Hector would send expensive bouquets to schoolgirls. The roses arrived in classrooms. There was so little time left.

After Hector's second wife was slain, there were 5,300 reported murders, 1,600 in Juarez alone, but there were many more unreported as Hector ordered policemen's corpses and the corpses of his former friends dissolved in acid. Meanwhile, his women closed their eyes to murder and torture, even as Elena heard men crying like children in far rooms of the mansion. The women she met desired wealth more than they valued life. Death as a rich woman was preferable to living as a poor one.

In the hidden mansion, nestled in the mountains, her sapphire earrings were heavy. Her long hair was pulled back with diamond clasps. After several nights with Hector, she resigned herself to long salon sessions, manicures, pedicures, hair treatments. The old man gave her a closet full of designer clothes and satchels full of jewels. He sent money to her family. He bought her parents a house that she would never see, never be allowed to enter.

To those who had known Elena in Georgia, she was not Miss Sinaloa. She was only a lovely immigrant. Most people in the United States blamed Elena's status on her culture and thought it had nothing to do with their homeland. Regardless, the Lyon family felt that Elena was connected to them.

Unlike decades of church sermons on the saving grace of the Christian god, she opened the eyes of the Lyon family. For the first time, the men, women, and children finally saw each other as they really were. Elena gave the Lyons the gift of perspective. Through fear and wisdom, the Lyons sensed that gift was bought with blood.

✢ ✢ ✢

At night when the Lyon children were sleeping, Elena retraced her footsteps, wondering how often she had profited from violence.

She felt guilty about the life she once led, the fearful luxury.

In Mexico, as a young girl, long-stem roses terrified her. She never understood why more young women weren't afraid of what their mothers and sisters said women should have wanted. Growing up, she was shaped by competition. Pageants were everything. Crowns were the key and the door, the only way out.

Though it seemed like a fairy tale, the old codes that once protected women and children were falling away. Santa Muerte could not protect wives, girlfriends, and children, but she could bring painful death to torturers and hitmen. The corpses of beloved women were messages to and from powerful men, signals in bone and blood. The men's death would also be a message, but it was a message that was hidden from the living. She knew that suffering could go on beyond death. Many men wanted to send messages. Santa Muerte would come, a last companion, the only one who dared to touch the untouchable women and to comfort them at the time of their dying.

Sometimes Elena wondered if the women had made the right choice. Then, she realized there was no choice. There were no career options. There was only marriage or hunger, the pageant or poverty, the mansion on the mountain or the cardboard house on the plains – nothing in between. Miss Sinaloa's crown was the key to the mansion on the mountain, and the mansion was a prison. Slowly, she discovered the link between the promise of seduction and the threat of decapitation. Once she accepted the roses, there was no escape.

Santa Muerte overpowered her and revealed the last image.

It was always the same. Elena didn't know what to think when the national news confirmed the image's validity. As drug wars raged out of control on the Mexico border, just outside of Juarez was a desert of open graves. The mass graves were empty and dark with shadow — holes dug for people still alive.

✝ ✝ ✝

"Help us, help us!" The Lyon children woke, crying for Elena.

They assumed the fantastical stories Elena told them about the shadow family and Santa Muerte were real. Before bedtime, Elena spoke of police stations covered with bullets, thousands of pits and holes haloing the doorways and windows. She had seen women die with severed noses hidden in bloody hair. Always it was the same: in dreams after violence, the Virgin of Guadalupe appeared, but she could never get rid of the dusty scent of cash packets that had touched her clothing and hair. Only Santa Muerte could avenge the shadow family.

Elena told the children tales of a queen living in luxury and fear. The king was a monster named Hector. His only enemy was Santa Muerte, who disguised herself as a dead woman. Every Tuesday, palace servants decorated the queen's long, fake fingernails with painted marijuana leaves. But no, Elena never said that word. She never said *marijuana*. She only said *bright green leaves*, everywhere painted on her fingernails and toenails, golden jewelry in the shape of *leaves*. The *leaves* were like flames behind the tiny black-and-white portraits of Jesús Malverde.

The Lyon children had no idea how Elena came to them, but they loved her as they loved Santa Muerte. Elena would never let the children kiss or hug her. Until Santa Muerte came for Elena, she would always be untouchable because Hector's bloodstained hands had claimed her.

✦ ✦ ✦

The Lyons sought each other out, longing only to be close. They realized how fragile life was, yet dreamed of Santa Muerte. The children whispered of the shadow family upon waking.

✦ ✦ ✦

Detectives escorted the Lyons to the police station just four blocks away from the enormous red brick Baptist church. Kenneth and the children were held in separate interview rooms.

Kenneth had been thinking he was witnessing two actors rehearsing a summer play or street festival event. Then, he realized what he was seeing. Before the screams, the knife seemed unreal.

Elena's screams set Kenneth's nightmares into motion, fracturing hopes with the same violence that had caused him to break all the mirrors in his secluded country home.

He imagined Elena. He dreamed of taking Elena's place, of going back in time and becoming a victim. After his children told him Elena's stories, he prayed to Santa Muerte for forgiveness, and Santa Muerte began to invade his dreams.

*Elena,* he said, *Elena. I'm just like you.* He kept repeating. *Elena. Why?*

Then, he remembered the children and the sounds. A sudden and horrible silence had descended like rain upon the downtown streets. That silence was soon broken by another scream, the howl inside him that seemed to continue long after the sirens blared.

Kenneth found photographs of Elena with his children. He gently caressed the faces with his fingertips — or rather, he pressed the cold glass over the framed faces.

Beneath years of images, were unframed photographs of his former self, a younger Kenneth. It had been years since Kenneth had allowed a picture of himself to be taken. In the photographs, he saw the aging, imperfect man he had become.

In a process that would take almost a week, the interviews began with the Lyon children at the Child Advocacy Center. In these delicate matters, the child psychiatrist tried to extract all necessary information from the children while protecting them from the truths they revealed.

Standing behind a one-way glass window, the detectives observed the child psychiatrist speaking to the children, one by one. The psychiatrist, Dr. Julia Weiner, started with the youngest first, apparently believing that the four-year-old Moses would have the least patience for the process, which was more like a play date than an official interview.

Traumatized by the recent events, each child reacted quite differently to the questions posed. While playing games, Dr. Julia delicately talked about secrets, what secrets meant, and whether the Lyon children knew any secrets about their father or Elena.

"Yes, she has a secret," Moses whispered.

The detectives sat up in their chairs.

"Can you tell me her secret?" Julia asked.

"She's with Santa Muerte."

✛ ✛ ✛

The final interview session with the Lyon children involved a new doll designed by a detective named Adams. In fact, the detective had stayed up late the night before the interview, confounding his wife by sewing in his study, scraps of socks and old shirts strewn across the hardwood floor. The doll he stitched was neither male nor female and had no face or distinguishing features. It didn't have to, according to Kenneth's description of the murderer. The detective sewed the doll into a black dress and black mask and cut a miniature machete shape out of cardboard from a cereal box, then wrapped the cardboard in shiny foil. Working from the sketches that matched the descriptions Kenneth had provided, Adams was satisfied that he had created a close replica of the murderer. Now, all that was left to do was to put the new doll into the children's hands and to see what games they might play.

Dr. Julia went along with the idea, after formally stating her objections to the detectives. Saying that she would not be held responsible if the Lyon children began to have nightmares, Julia slowly reached for the doll and stroked the foil of the paper knife. "Why are you doing this to them?" she asked Detective Adams.

He clutched at the doll he had spent hours creating and panicked, thinking of all the time he had lost if the doll were never used. "You know why, Julia," he said.

Julia cradled the masked doll like an infant as she walked into the interview room where all four of the Lyon children waited in silence.

Moses reached for the masked doll and began playing, recreating the crime scene with blocks and *Barbies*. The other children helped. While watching the children play, Dr. Julia read into the makeshift scene while referring to Detective Adams's notes on Kenneth Lyon's eyewitness account.

Near the church in daylight, mature oak trees sheltered the swept alley beside the renovated playground. The Lyon children played on the large red slide that dwarfed the bucket swings. Elena, having just left the children to grab a cup of coffee and four ice waters in paper cups, exited the coffee shop around 12:35 PM. Her screams were heard shortly after. In all, the police located five witnesses who had first-hand knowledge of the bizarre and grisly scene. Kenneth Lyon's children each saw fragments of the attack through the oak trees and the cyclone fence. Kenneth absorbed a chilling view of Elena's final moments through the high windows of his office overlooking the playground and the alley. Later, detectives would realize that Kenneth

practically had a private theater of exclusive picture windows —
the way the huge panes of glass overlooked the murder site and the
streets of downtown.

✛ ✛ ✛

When Elena suddenly met the shadow family, she kept searching for
Santa Muerte. Slowly, the shadow family led her. Lovely women were
found in trunks of cars with letters carved into their flesh, the letters
filled with blue ink.

# Longtime Passing

Dawn struck sorghum fields edging highways. On Barbed Wire Road, my pickup stuttered over cattle guards. Distant wheat glinted golden in the sun shining on metal-roof barns. Sparrows flittered by oaks. Horse flies sparkled like vintage black Cadillacs parked near the garage housing Uncle's infamous car collection. As Becca adjusted the radio, I remembered, long ago, Uncle speeding down the highway. Chasing me in his classic Cadillac, he seemed mysterious and distant like a stranger.

Coming home to Uncle felt peculiar after so many years. I fled Texas just after graduating high school because my abortion happened around the time of Becca's miscarriage. We had grown up together playing dolls, and she couldn't understand a girl not wanting a baby. When she told me exactly how she felt about my choice, I tried to explain. Though we both lived with the secret of being Uncle's girls, we didn't speak again for sixteen years, until she called to say Uncle, now sixty-eight-years-old, had been in a medically induced coma for three days and wouldn't live much longer.

A bull lurked behind barbed wire. Two horses, wobbly from eating fermented orchard fruit, cantered to us near Uncle's stables. I asked Victor, the ranch hand, if it would be okay for us to ride the horses.

In the saddle, I felt natural and free. On her horse, Becca beamed at me. "Race you to the orchard," she said.

Breathless, we galloped to Uncle's gleaming peach trees and began picking ripe fruit while still seated on the horses. "My god," I whispered. When I bit into that first peach, my mouth ached. It literally hurt me to chew it. Fresh peach, just picked from the tree, held a certain quality. It tasted different. It felt different. It was so pleasurable to the tongue that it caused pain. The peaches in the orchard were bursting with flavor, but imperfectly shaped with spatters of what looked like freckles and the occasional dark hole from worm. They were smaller than store-bought peaches, but for me, the choice was obvious — taste and flavor beat looks and shape any day.

"Hear that?" Becca asked, chewing. "The orchard is alive."

"It is?"

"That buzzing? I can feel it."

"Be careful," I said because the orchard was full of wasps and bees. We were on their territory, and I didn't want to anger them. The buzz filled the air, electric. I worried. What if the bees swarmed? What if a wasp stung? We were invading their territory, the orchard a home to thousands. The sweetness inviting stings, we moved on to the tunnel to search for the rest of Uncle's girls.

✦ ✦ ✦

We knew just how to find the tunnel beneath the fields. Its opening waited, a dark hole in the ravine reached by climbing down the hill. Where the runnel enveloped the concrete and metal drainage, rocks and trees harnessed a channel for sound, allowing words to travel so that voices seemed altered.

As young girls angry for reasons we didn't understand, we screamed obscenities into the tunnel all during our childhood on the ranch. We screamed terrible things into the tunnel for years, releasing emotions too dark for us to process. "You evil bitch!" Becca and I screamed to hear the echo answer in darkness. "You monster! Get out of here! Why are you hiding from us? We know what you've done. We know what happened to you. Show yourself!"

Because of the voice we heard calling back to us through the tunnel, we named her the Woman of Echoes. Our fathers teased there was a real woman in the tunnel, waiting for Uncle, who had a history of doomed romance, leaving a trail of broken-hearted girls leading to the Woman of Echoes. She gave us shivers. Her echoes traveled long and far after our voices faded.

Hearing the woman in the tunnel after all these years was like hearing the voice of an old friend. When Becca and I were kids, we used to joke that the woman was waiting for Uncle. Our joking hid our terror. We feared the tunnel was Shelia's grave. Before Shelia, Becca's father and my father and the other men in our family used to sit around, joking about "Uncle's girls." After family dinners on the ranch, the men drank whiskey while speaking of Uncle's girls and smoking cigars on the back porch facing the fields.

In those days, before we became like them, Uncle's girls followed Becca and me on the property where they hid, waiting for us in the shadows.

✣ ✣ ✣

Searching for Uncle's girls, I witnessed drunken birds intoxicated with fallen fruit. Drunken birds, like drunken horses, were among my favorite things. Drunken horses befriended me in childhood in my Uncle's orchard where the fruit fermented on loamy ground after summer rains. Horses who roamed there often got drunk by gorging on those peaches. Drunken horses, like drunken people, can be clumsy but lovable. Open, relaxed, affable, they wander curious routes and meander in lovely ways.

Until I was a teenager, I wanted to live like a drunken horse in the orchard. Before Uncle's girls began startling horses in shadows, the ranch was peaceful and scenic. Uncle bought an oil field that made him wealthy. A millionaire and eligible bachelor, Uncle was picky about his girls, though the ranch was his passion.

Despite having flings, he only fell in love once with a deer hunter who leased land from him. The two of them started spending time together, weekends walking the vast wooded acres she had leased. An expert markswoman, she captured the heart of an inexperienced hunter. She could stalk, kill, dress, and butcher prized game. She was highly educated and highly competitive, a heart surgeon, but also wild and rugged enough to live off Uncle's land for days.

The summer they finally announced their engagement, Shelia was trailing a 170-class buck in velvet. Carefully patterning the deer, she announced she wouldn't marry Uncle until she shot the buck and had its head mounted over his bed. It had to be a perfect, clean shot. She watched the buck in Uncle's fields in the evenings, identifying its bedding and feeding areas. When the buck disappeared during the rut, she disappeared with it.

Uncle was investigated by the local police, but there was no evidence against him, no body, no charges.

In the months after Shelia's disappearance, just before their marriages fell apart, my parents began arguing with Becca's parents. They conversed in whispers. My father told my mother and Becca's parents that Uncle had been drinking whiskey and saying he shot Shelia by accident, thinking she was a deer. He buried her on his ranch, camouflaging the grave.

Becca and I started shadowing Uncle, who drunkenly walked alone for hours on his land. He kept returning to the tunnel, calling into it, day after day. The Woman of Echoes answered.

Over the years, Uncle dated many girls, always much younger than him. We saw their silhouettes weaving through the oak trees, their shadows sitting in parked Cadillacs.

The tunnel was large enough for us to enter, but we never crawled inside it. There were things we searched for but never wanted to find: whispers of wind through the orchard, breath of fermenting peaches, hair of dazzling sun slipping into the tunnel.

✛ ✛ ✛

"Becca," I called. "Becca!" My horse wasn't following hers, and her horse was taking her in the opposite direction, toward the trees that led to the tunnel. My horse sauntered toward the north side of the orchard, the cherry trees near the martin houses.

"Look, I'll meet you back over there," she called, the distance between us growing.

"What? Over where?"

"There," I thought she pointed toward the windmills, but I couldn't be sure because my horse suddenly raised her neck, neighed, and kicked up her front hooves. I held on as she started galloping. "Becca?" By then, Becca fell far behind, and the wind was once again whipping my hair into a frenzied mane.

By the time our horses slowed, Becca said my hair looked like spun sugar.

Where were we? I thought we knew every inch of the property. We had visited Uncle's ranch so many times in childhood and explored the land countless times, and yet suddenly, nothing looked familiar. Everything seemed strange.

"Is it just me," asked Becca, "or is that tree different?"

"I've never seen that before on this property," I said, noting it was a large 100-year-old oak. I would have seen it before, if it had been on Uncle's ranch. I began searching for anything familiar — any landmark that could provide a sense of direction, so we would know which way to go. The horses still had no interest in guiding us back to the stables, and since they caused this mess, I was less inclined to trust them as guides.

"Becca, do you have your phone?" I asked.

"No," she said. "Do you?"

I shook my head, realizing I had left mine in my pickup.

If the horses knew the way back, they would eventually take us home when they got hungry. To the stables. That was the secret hope I was clinging to, that a horse could save its rider. But we were all suffering from heat exhaustion, galloping while baking in the sun with no water.

We galloped more, speeding through waves of wind. Insects hit my face and teeth, my mouth and nose gritty with dirt. Corn fields, wheat fields, gardens of okra and tomatoes, roaming goats and sheep, cows sleeping beneath the shade of trees as cow birds scattered in our wake. We passed rusted tractors and a graveyard of cars before finally racing a dry dusty road near the scrub trees. The road, rutted, jutted through the scraggily grass along fallow fields. "We are so lost," I said, slowing upon seeing a house, so longstanding its windows were gone and the wood rotting where the roof was falling beside the crumbling chimney.

Since we had not seen the highway or any signs of civilization, except for the wheat and corn and animals and the graveyard of tractors, I worried.

"I feel sick," said Becca.

My thighs bruised and blistered from riding, I was thirsty and hungry. I had eaten nothing all day but those few peaches. We were in a mess of trouble. "I'll see if I can't find some water," I said.

"Good," Becca said. "I'm parched."

Becca wobbled off her horse and fell on the dirt.

✢ ✢ ✢

I rode around the trees several times before I located a larger pond near a small pond and a medium pond downhill and covered in cattails. Once the horse realized where I was leading it, it started walking faster. When it finally reached the edge of the pond and lowered its head to drink, the horse inhaled the water. How thirsty that horse was! It drank desperately, then long and steady. I led it back to the old, abandoned house and tied it to a tree.

"Becca ... Becca?" I called. She peeked out of an empty window frame, her hair wild. Something inside the house crashed, and I heard her say, "It's hot in here."

I approached Becca's horse, panting and slick with white sweat. I said, "Let me take you to a nice pond where you can have a drink." Becca's horse seemed to understand me because it allowed me to lead it toward the pond, despite its exhaustion. When it saw the water from a distance, it started galloping, again. At the pond's edge, it threw me into the water.

✝ ✝ ✝

A shiny black Cadillac drove down the dirt road and emerged gleaming from the dust. I would recognize it anywhere — the jewel of Uncle's car collection.

I hopped back on Becca's horse and headed toward the Cadillac while hollering and waving. The Cadillac slowed to a stop, but just as I got close to it, it drove off again.

Maybe someone had stolen one of Uncle's Cadillacs, or maybe a farmhand had taken it for a joyride? Whatever the reason, the sun was setting when I rode back to Becca and heard the Cadillac's horn. The Cadillac made a U-turn, stirring the dust.

The Cadillac reached a point on the road ahead of me. The window rolled down. When I saw Uncle sitting in the driver's seat, I swallowed hard. It had been around two decades since I had seen him, so it was no wonder he didn't recognize me.

"Hello there, beautiful," Uncle said. "You're trespassing. Unless I'm mistaken, that horse you're riding isn't yours." He paused, squinting. "Trina, is that you? My stars!"

"Becca's here, too," I said.

"No kidding? Why didn't you girls stop by the house or call me?"

"The family said you were ... unable to visit."

"Why the hell did they tell you that?"

"They said you were in the hospital?"

"Don't listen to rumors," he said. "I've been expanding the ranch. Just take this dirt road up the direction I came. The house is a ten-minute ride away."

"Ten minutes? We've been riding for hours."

He laughed. "You got turned around. Happens to the best of us."

I blew Uncle a kiss and took off riding toward the abandoned house as the Cadillac made another U-turn and drove away.

As soon as I reached the abandoned house, I went inside to find Becca sleeping on the floor. "Becca," I whispered, "wake up. Come on."

Becca groaned. We limped to the horses and coaxed them to the dirt road on a rather brief journey. The horses seemed uneasy when we saw Uncle's ranch house in the distance, the clay-colored stone glistening in fading light.

Becca and I ran, muscles aching. The door, unlocked, swung smoothly on old hinges. Inside the house, nothing was as it had been in our childhood. It was filthy, stacked with junk, piles of old newspapers and magazines on the tile, chairs, tables, and sofa. The rooms stank of mildew and rotting food. The toilets weren't flushed, and the house hadn't been cleaned in likely a decade.

Becca ran for the nearest faucet in a guest bathroom, which wasn't working. She stumbled toward the kitchen blocked off by garbage. Clawing her way through piles of trash, she reached the kitchen sink and wedged her head between filthy pots to drink straight from the tap, flies swarming.

The front door opened, and Victor, the ranch foreman, stepped gingerly into the entryway. "Becca? Trina?" he called. "Oh, shit."

I almost cried. Uncle would have never wanted strangers or employees to see his place like this. He must have been ashamed.

"He wouldn't want the rest of the family — or anyone, even strangers or employees — to see it like this," I said. "You remember the way it was?"

"Alright, leave it to us," said Becca, as if cleaning Uncle's house would be penitence for neglecting to visit or check on him all these years. Maybe he would forgive us without our having to explain what took us so long to come back for a visit.

I said to Victor, "When was the last time you saw him?"

"A few weeks ago, before the ambulance came," said Victor.

"He's getting better now?"

"Honey, as far as I know, he never left that hospital. He's not even conscious and hasn't been for days. He could go anytime."

Becca was staring at me.

"Sorry," I said. "Long day."

"Where have you two been all this time?" asked Victor. "I was waiting for you. I went all over the property looking for you."

"We got turned around," said Becca.

Becca and I cleared some space in one of the guest bedrooms, just enough so the bed was accessible. Underneath all the newspapers and magazines, the sheets were clean, though stale. The bathroom was the hardest room to deal with, as it was the guest bathroom and seldom used. There was no water in the toilet since it had not been flushed for too long. The sink was full of wrapped bars of discount soap. I took them out of the sink and gave a bar to Becca. She sniffed. "Still good." Then, I held my breath and pushed the handle on the toilet. Becca and I hooted and high-fived each other as the bowl filled with fresh water and stopped right where it should. The shower was full of toys — our old toys. We removed the dusty dolls with tangled hair and the disintegrating teddy bears and stuffed rabbits with deteriorated fur.

We turned on the shower. It worked! Hot water started flowing, steaming up the mirrors.

Becca and I stripped off our dirty clothes and jumped in the shower, just like we had as girls. We were women now, with women's bodies. We gazed at each other for a moment, as if noting the changes, then each placed a hand on each other's belly and stared at each other in silence, acknowledging old hurts, what we had lost. The hot water felt good. After the shower, Becca crawled onto the bed without bothering to turn down the blankets. She slept under towels.

Carefully, I found a trail to the kitchen. I tried not to gag because of the spoiled food. I searched for glasses and found two to rinse in the sink. I filled one with cool water and gulped. Then, I filled both glasses with water and made my way back to the guest room. "Here," I said, handing Becca a glass of water. "Oh," she said. "Oh." She drank frantically, greedily, choking, spilling the water down her chin and neck, soaking the sheets.

"More," she whispered. I gave her the other glass of water, and she gulped it down, then I began refilling the glasses in the shower. We drank three more glasses of water each before falling into a deep sleep under the towels.

We woke to search the closets. In the hall closets, we discovered bleach, glass cleaner, a vacuum, dust cloths, mops, a broom and pan, Lysol, and ant killer.

We started stacking piles of trash onto the back porch and tossing trash into the drained concrete pool, cracked right down the center. We filled the empty pool with soiled clothes, pounds and pounds of old magazines and newspapers, spoiled food, and filthy bedding. We threw out an old mattress blackened with mold and trash bag after trash bag of fast-food wrappers and used paper plates.

Victor stood near the pool, now brimming with trash. I thought he might get upset, since he had been keeping the grounds so pristine. "Good," he said. "I'll order one of those rented dumpsters and haul this away."

Some carpets were egregiously stained, as were the sofas and chairs, but we got the rest of the house sparkling, free of rubbish, cleared and smelling refreshingly of pine.

By the time evening descended over the fields, Becca and I were weak with accomplishment.

The doorbell rang. I answered. It was Victor, looking bashful. "I just got word from the hospital your uncle passed this evening."

The house looked clean, so much like the beautiful home it once was, our sanctuary, but Uncle would never see it again. I said, "We did a good thing, even if he never knew."

"Don't you think it's weird," said Becca as Victor left us in Uncle's house.

"I don't want to talk about it," I said.

Becca's cellphone rang, and she answered it.

"It's Victor," she said. She was listening to whatever he was saying, responding in monotone. Then she looked at me.

"What?" I asked.

Becca spoke into her cell phone. "Could you ask Trina?"

Taking the cellphone from Becca, I asked, "What's up?"

"Are you two planning on attending the funeral?" asked Victor. "We'll have the wake at his house, since it's clean. People are already asking to see you."

"Who?" I asked.

"A woman," said Victor, "showed up with a bunch of girls who claim to know your uncle. She says there's something she needs to tell you."

"Okay," I said.

"Here she is," said Victor.

I held the cellphone to my ear and heard a woman's voice. I recognized it right away. It was the woman in the tunnel. The Woman of Echoes was hollering back everything Becca and I had ever said to her; all we had ever screamed into the tunnel. When she finally stopped screaming, I heard bees buzzing in the orchard.

# Ducky

Tripping over high heels, curlers, and pastel gowns, I snuck into my father's house and found it boobytrapped with paisley evening dresses. These dresses haunted me because Mother would never wear them again. They were ghosts of her youth, ethereal yet stylish, like the woman she once was. Attempting to avoid the gowns my father thought I might wear, I felt guilty. Maybe I was a bad daughter? In helping my father to mourn, maybe I should have attempted to become Mother, or at least more like she was. Looking past low, square heels with Mary Jane straps, just like doll's shoes, in shades of baby pink, lime green, mustard yellow, and sky blue, I got a shock.

"When did you get this new floor?" I asked my father in the smoky little kitchen. That Sunday afternoon, several months after Mother's death, I delivered groceries for our dinner — dog food for Ducky and, for my father and me, steak and new potatoes with ham-hocked greens. I prepared our simple meal in the grease-stained kitchen with vintage avocado wallpaper coated with grime.

"What floor?" My father asked in his kooky voice, the one he used when he had sloshed down one Coors too many.

Groceries spilled out of the ripped bag, which I clutched, hopelessly, while watching my father stumble toward me in just his boots and stained powder-blue boxer shorts. Hand sewn, printed with faded unicorns, so threadbare as to border on translucent, his shorts should have been outlawed for indecent exposure. The material was older than I was. I thought, *respect your elders.* Trying not to stare, I wondered how long the stain had been there. My mother never would have allowed him to walk around in stained shorts.

A hand-rolled cigarette dangled from his paper-thin lips as he squinted beneath thick square-framed glasses. Having recently lost his wife (my mother) and most of his friends to cancer (all smokers, like him), my father, a retired mechanical engineer and devout Baptist, lived alone in a Gold Medallion, full electric, brick ranch house on ten acres of stocked ponds in a small town jam-packed with churches in rural Alabama.

In Birmingham, about a half hour away by highway, I lived with my girlfriend, working nights at the hospital with her, but made sure to visit my father at least once a week.

"This new flooring looks expensive," I said, staring down at the gray spackle.

A muffled quack bellowed beneath the wobbly kitchen table burned by cigarettes, plates of ashes like black snow.

"Ducky," I said. "Here, Ducky."

Opening a bag of dog food, I tossed kibbles onto crusted linoleum, waited for Ducky to emerge. Blue eyes and white feathers gleaming, he could barely move his fat ass. Morbidly obese, suffering from the munchies, staggering drunkenly, he waddled, an overfed ivory-feathered American Pekin from a family of domestic ducks reared principally for meat.

"This little guy," my father said, "don't know what I'd do without him."

"No telling," I said.

"Care for a smoke?" my father asked.

"Yes," I said, but then realized he was talking to Ducky.

✝✝✝

My father started giving Ducky cigarettes when Ducky was a duckling. These were special cigarettes, not the kind humans smoke, but much smaller and thinner, shaped like hollow paper needles of hash. My father made them by hand, cutting cigarette paper, using a miniature roller. Ducky had to be trained to smoke these cigarettes, which my father connected to a homemade breathing apparatus, a tiny respirator and beak tube. Ducky began to crave cigarettes, to request them with a special quack, deeper, louder, more prolonged the more he smoked. He had a pronounced smoker's quack.

Because of Ducky, my father survived in unsanitary conditions, a firetrap of old newspapers near smacks of hardened duck poot splattered like a Jackson Pollock painting. Mounds of cracker boxes, feed sacks, dog food, water bottles, and children's tub toys were thickly bespattered. The house became a giant splatter painting in gray, black, and white, splotches stretching from floors to walls to ceilings.

I could only do so much to tackle the worst biohazards — clogged toilets, bathtubs of stagnant water, half-smoked joints in beds, toilets, and tubs. The sofa so crusted and hardened, I was afraid to sit down.

"Don't you dare touch it," my father warned whenever I threatened to hire a cleaning lady. "As Pollock said, *Painting is self-discovery. Every good artist paints what he is.*"

My father encouraged Ducky to let his art come through, saying for Ducky, as for Jackson Pollock, technique was just a means of arriving at a statement. What that statement was, I never quite knew, but years later, after my father died, I began touring galleries and collecting books on Pollock's work. That's how I discovered certain walls in my father's house were near replicas of *Autumn Rhythm,*

*The Deep, Convergence,* and *Number 1 (Lavender Mist).*

"All goes to prove," my father once said, "animals can be artists just as artists can be animals."

Like Pollock, Ducky was an abstract expressionist, creating a unique style of drip painting, his leavings transforming my father's house into what the neighbors deemed "a work of art," what the city called "a public health hazard."

Late at night, my father sat in his living room while rolling one tiny joint after another, attempting to keep the neighbors away from the windows. Fanfare made Ducky nervous. He was highly paranoid, didn't like photographs. Being a recluse, Ducky was shy of strangers with cameras, though he had a big following in town, his own channel on YouTube until PETA shut it down.

If by chance Ducky fell asleep, my father and I were careful not to wake him. Rolling tiny duck joints in silence, my father and I, once estranged, grew closer. Having always been close to my mother, who was once my best friend, I never understood my father, or perhaps had never bothered to understand him until our Ducky days. I finally got to know my father late in life thanks to Ducky, who blew smoke out his ass, lifting his tailfeathers and webbed feet, flipping elegantly to expel gas as abstract art.

Ducky was, of course, a damaged duckling, "defective." A rare physical deformity and a problem in his hatching led to developmental anomalies in his internal organs, his plumbing, as my father would say. Ducky's physical defect gave him the gift of smoking in his unique way. Of course, as with most smokers, the activity that gave him the most pleasure began to shorten his life.

The house would eventually be condemned because Ducky was a poot bandit, and like most ducks, could not be housetrained. The outlandish shits he took, blowing them out his smoking cloaca, splattered everywhere, even in my father's scraggly hair, since my father and Ducky slept in the same bed.

Ducky rarely left the house, for safety reasons, but inside the house, he roamed free, pooting prolifically. My father began living in filth for the same reason we initially tried to craft a tiny duck bong carved of horn — love of family, art, animals, and Texas tea. The pipe was a failure, and it was complicated to teach a duck how to get a decent bong going. When we switched to mooking, some people considered what we were doing animal cruelty, but Ducky had a better life than any human, the life of an average duck denied him because of his deformity, making it impossible for him to swim, run, or fly. A crippled duckling probably wouldn't have lived long in the wild. Nevertheless, some people thought what my father and I did was wrong.

After what happened, I don't believe in keeping ducks as pets or allowing animals to smoke marijuana, except for medical reasons. Keeping a duck as a pet should be a crime, and is in many cities, for reasons clear to anyone who has ever tried. I've come to believe it's morally wrong, unless a person wants to devote ten to twenty years to caring for a duck. My father was one of the few who truly had the desire.

At night, we sat in his living room, rolling one tiny cigarette after another. If, by chance, Ducky fell asleep, "shhhh," my father said.

I began to realize Ducky understood my father as his pet and his parent, and my father was fine with this, but I worried they were co-dependent.

✛ ✛ ✛

When Ducky had a conniption, he had two choices — smoke the cigarette or stop breathing. Eventually, he grew stronger, more used to his lifestyle of handcrafted motorized miniature wheelchairs and remote-control toy tugboats. As he smoked customized joints of the finest quality medicinal marijuana, my father feared Ducky might get cancer like my mother, a lifetime smoker who, in her last days, had needed a respirator to breathe. Mother's respirator gave my father the idea of crafting the respirator cigarette, for Ducky.

Ducky imprinted my father's image upon his heart in a way I never had imprinted it upon my own. Closer to my father than I was, Ducky loved my father more than I ever could. If the feeling was mutual, Ducky was a threat to my father's mental and physical health.

My father was convinced Ducky needed to smoke to relieve chronic pain. That's why he created the breathing apparatus, but in creating it, my father created another addict, another beloved chronic smoker he was in danger of losing. This was why my father designed the miniature motorized wheelchair and the duck-sized tugboat, so Ducky could smoke while following him throughout the house, even in the bathtub.

✛ ✛ ✛

A strong and defiant woman, my mother lost her battle with lung cancer, smoking to the very end. That's why my father gave Ducky a blissful existence, the kind he always wanted for my mother but could never manage.

My father found Ducky after my mother's funeral, when he happened upon the malformed duckling caught in its shell while hatching. Hearing the duckling's cries in a feed-store dumpster, he dived in to rescue it.

"Look, here, Loren," my father said, cradling Ducky in his palms. Ducky was tiny — downy, slimy, covered with dried egg and blood. Shell attached to his bottom half wouldn't fall, though the duckling's head and much of its upper body had already broken through.

"What's that?" I whispered.

My father moved his hands into sunlight behind the feed store and splayed his fingers to reveal the encrusted creature nesting between his palms.

"Dad," I said. "It's suffering."

"They dumped him into the dumpster — alive."

"Put it out of its misery. Please?"

"What some call misery," my father said, "others call life."

It was a speech he had given many times about my mother in her last days when the only thing that made her feel better was the cigarette my father rolled for her by hand.

My father cooed at the duckling. Covered in bird scat and feathers from dumpster diving, my father stank, but he smiled for the first time in weeks while the little damaged duckling wheezed and quacked in his big trembling hands, so full of gentleness.

"Come on," he said. "Let's go inside and talk to the owner."

"No," I said, wondering if what he was doing would only lead to more pain. I wondered if in losing my mother, after caring for her in a hopeless situation, he needed to care for another creature doomed to suffer. What could he be thinking, inviting this hurt?

The duckling, with sweet blue eyes and a perfectly formed head and upper body, was tragically deformed. It had been tossed into the dumpster for a reason. It shivered in my father's large-veined, callused hands. I could see from the determined look in my father's eyes he was set on taking it home.

Because my father was now the child in our relationship, I became the mother. If a woman lives long enough, if her father enjoys longevity, this is bound to happen.

"These might be its last moments," I whispered. "Let it go?"

"How?" he whispered.

I thought of my mother, the way my father held her after she died and didn't want to let the ambulance take her body.

"Hank," my father said, approaching the feed-store owner. "Could I purchase this duckling?"

As if swallowing a bug, Hank gasped, asking, "Where did you find it?"

"The trash," I said. "Your dumpster out back."

"Damned shame," Hank said, and my father started kissing the duckling.

"Couldn't agree more," I said.

"Why do I even have employees?"

"To end its suffering?" I asked.

"We have lots of healthy ducklings to choose from," said Hank, lighting a cigarette, casting a glance at his son, the assistant manager, John.

"No," my father said. "I'll take the duckling. How much do you want for him?"

I sighed, watching Hank smoke. His lungs were probably like my mother's, or would be in time — damaged, enlarged air sacks causing breathlessness, doing nothing to decrease the craving for cigarettes that caused emphysema in the first place.

"Jesus," I whispered.

The little duckling stopped crying, drifted to sleep in my father's hands.

"Couldn't sell it," Hank said. "Johnny, why don't you do like I told you?"

Hank puffed his cigarette, and John smiled in an embarrassed way, adjusting his cap.

"Wait," my father said, stepping back, clutching the sleeping duckling to his chest as he stared down at John's steel-toed boots. "Give me a minute," he said.

I sighed, pretending I was smoking a cigarette. I had quit smoking only months before, to fulfill my mother's dying wish, knowing I would miss it for the rest of my life.

My father told me to pay for three bags of feed and a warming light, then to unlock the car for John to load the bags. "I'll just go to the trees to smoke," he said. I stood with Hank, watching my father steal the duckling in his hat.

"That's that," Hank said. "Sorry to hear about your mother, Loren."

"What do we owe you?" I asked.

"Not a damn thing," he said, lighting another cigarette while walking away.

✢ ✢ ✢

Being so young, living away from his own kind, Ducky came to recognize my father as not only his parent but also an object of habitual trust. Afraid to be without my father, even for short periods of time, Ducky quacked hysterically whenever my father left him to go to the kitchen or bathroom. My father began to carry Ducky everywhere in the pocket of his robe, even when he went to the toilet. He showered with Ducky and snuck him into banks, grocery stores, and doctor's offices, resting Ducky inside his jacket.

Ducky slept on the pillow my mother once slept upon, and my father focused the heat lamp to keep Ducky warm.

Since Ducky was tiny and covered in scabby shell, we thought we were just keeping him comfortable, that he could slip away any day. This was why my father fed Ducky by hand and let Ducky sleep in the bed with him. We didn't know about imprinting then, the reason why Ducky quacked mournfully and struggled to follow my father.

Ducky was eating and drinking well, but I didn't think he would survive because shell was still attached to his body, the crust along his translucent belly.

"What's that, Dad?" I asked.

"Shell."

"I know. Why is it there?"

On his belly shell, ragged yolk dried in blood.

"Maybe we should pull it off?" I asked, offering tweezers.

"He's not ready."

Ducky squawked, rolling off the pillow. Still small enough to fit in my hands, he only trusted my father, so I gave up on tweezers.

Days later, a twisted webbed foot emerged from the crusted shell, and my father created a tiny swimming pool, a mixing bowl filled with warm tap water. Ducky swam for hours, exhausting himself so he had to be occasionally lifted out of the water. I noticed something floating beneath Ducky as he peddled. It was shell, no longer attached, bobbing in the water as Ducky quacked. Soon, more shell washed away, the last bits falling onto his pillow as he slept through the night.

As Ducky matured, my father informed me Ducky couldn't walk or take care of himself or be alone or go outside and seemed to be in chronic pain.

"Ducky needs your mother's medicine," he said, and I suspected he was talking about himself, his own pain, the aliments of aging and smoking, the depression he attempted to hide.

"What?" I asked, realizing that not only would I not be getting my mother's marijuana, but my father would waste it on a duck.

"I just need to find a way to get him to smoke it," my father said.

"You're kidding?"

"I never kid about pain, kid."

I had already planned to appropriate mother's medical marijuana. I thought it would go to waste in her dusty jewelry box, but soon discovered there was even more of it in her pantyhose drawer.

To teach Ducky, my father and I smoked cigarette after cigarette, demonstrating what had to be done. Ducky couldn't hold the joint properly.

"This is wrong," my father said. The more my father smoked, the more he reverted to the thick accent of his roots. I was delighted because, for once, I agreed with him.

I said, "I just want to smoke with you, Dad."

"No, I mean these roaches are the wrong size. He needs small ones to fit his beak."

My head crashed down to the pillow, launching Ducky so he landed on my face. He quacked. I coughed, trying to breathe, inhaling feathers.

"Careful, careful," my father said, rolling little cigarettes, as I lifted my head before setting Ducky back on the pillow.

These new cigarettes almost worked, but not quite, so we stayed up all night fashioning a duck bong carved from horn and attached to a respirator with a clip to help Ducky hold the bong in his beak. I worried for Ducky: would smoking be good for him? But mostly, I worried for my father: would he lose his only friend, after losing his only love? I could still hear her voice, one of the few times Mother talked to me about her smoking. "This stuff keeps me sane and happy," she said. "I'd say it's a great drug, but obviously not very healthy."

Within hours of my father's adjusting the tiny clip bong, Ducky caught on. He smoked joint after joint until his pain seemed gone. It was a miracle — the only miracle I had ever witnessed. Or, so it seemed. He even began to walk, hobbling over pillows until the tubes in his respirator tangled around his crippled limbs and had to be unwound. Eventually, my father and Ducky began to smoke together, leaving me out, no longer needing me for company or having any weed to spare. Whenever Ducky's cigarette ran out, he nestled into the crook of my father's neck to breathe in my father's smoke.

It went on like that for almost two years, until Ducky's vitality began to slip away.

"My best friend is dying," my father said, not long before he lost Ducky, who was not moving or quacking the way he used to.

✛ ✛ ✛

When Ducky died, my father had him cremated and kept his ashes in a cigar box near my mother's urn, beside Ducky's pillow, my mother's pillow. For days, I was picking clumps of duck poot out of my father's greasy hair. "Leave me alone," he said. "I just want sleep."

My father didn't leave the house or get a new duckling. He became a recluse. Five months later, he died peacefully in bed, a full ashtray on his nightstand.

Finding my father's eldest sister, a lifetime smoker, I confronted her at his wake.

There was nothing I could say.

"Cigarette?" she asked.

"Sure," I said.

She passed me the soft pack and let me borrow her silver lighter.

# The Open Invitation

Geb Lobos lived on the east side of Juniper Hills, near the woods, a flood zone rife with creeks, not far from the intersection of Chester and Willis Streets, where the tractor trailer accident happened in the late 1970s. Single and now in his mid-fifties, he worked as a pharmacist. In the evenings, he sat on the swing on his screened porch facing his backyard, overlooking greenspace edging the woods.

On the other side of the trees, Craven House stood empty in the misty hollow. Geb played harmonica. Songbirds flew from tree to tree. He searched the woods and remembered Karen Craven. It had been about three months since he saw her. She lived in the house in the hollow with her mother. Geb would often walk through his backyard to the little trail through the woods to visit them both. They expected him around dinner time each evening. He never arrived empty handed. He would bring a half pound of freshly ground coffee (dark roast), a bag of pecans in their shells, a little basket of fruit from his orchard, a jar of preserves, or a modestly priced bottle of wine, typically red.

Karen and her mother were good cooks, and when he moved into his house two decades ago, they gave him an open invitation to join them for dinner. Since the three of them enjoyed each other's company, he accepted the invitation every evening. After dinner, they sat out on the Cravens' porch, facing the darkening woods. Owls hooted. They gossiped and spoke of the weather and played cards. A little wine, a lot of laughter, and some cigar smoking invigorated most nights, if the mood struck. He played hymns on his harmonica and the women sang "Amazing Grace," their favorite song. Harmonizing and weaving, Karen's alto braided into her mother's soprano, their song echoing through the woods. Reaching perfect pitch gave him chills. When he looked at Karen, he was sure he loved her. Though he had first met her when she was a girl of fifteen, she was now past her prime. Admiring her mother, he saw the woman Karen would be, though he assumed Karen only viewed him as an old man. He had been thirty-five when she was fifteen, the year he moved into his house, alone. For decades, they had stayed up late together visiting, so by the time he walked home, alone, the woods were a deep dark. His little flashlight beam sliced the night.

The open invitation went on for years. He thought of marrying Karen but was in no hurry. Everything seemed as if it would keep going the way it was. Then, one evening, he walked the trail through the misty woods to find Craven house empty, dark, no women inside, no food cooking on the stove. He came back the next evening to find the house the same. He began to wonder if the women had gone on a trip together and had forgotten to inform him. It was a free country, after all, he reasoned, and he wasn't family. Maybe he had overstayed his welcome and they had grown weary of the open invitation. Leaving would be the easiest way to inform him without telling him. "It's a free country," he whispered to himself, again. They didn't owe him anything, even an explanation.

At night, he lay awake, imagining the women traveling to national parks to hike in forests and climb mountains. He hoped their trip was enjoyable. One day, he imagined, they would tell him about it, but he intended never to make a pest of himself again, to no longer impose upon them by coming to dinner every evening. Once they returned, things would be different. He would only come for dinner once in a while, just to make sure he wasn't imposing.

After several weeks, he began to worry and to wonder if something were amiss. Just to be sure, he decided to check their garage. He walked through the woods and approached Craven House. Standing on his tiptoes, he stared into the dusty windows of the garage. The car was gone. He was nearly satisfied, but as more days passed, he couldn't stay away from Craven House. One evening, around dinner time, he broke in through the patio door. Finding the house in perfect order, he felt ashamed and tried to cover his tracks by mending the pry marks on the door. He walked back home through the woods, alone, ate a can of beans, and went to bed.

That was three months ago, in May. Now, in August, Craven House was still empty. He missed Karen and her mother and wondered if they missed him. As the sky faded over the trees, he swung on his porch swing and played harmonica while thinking of them. He was sorry he had never kissed Karen, though he had often thought of doing so.

A shadow passed overhead — a large swooping darkness over the trees. He looked up at the lamppost just in time to see the red-tailed hawk landing on its perch, majestic. He stared at it, wanting to watch until it flew away. Focused on the hawk, he wasn't paying attention to other things. For instance, when he heard a soft scraping behind him, he ignored it. Another sound inside the house fell like footsteps, yet he only had eyes for the hawk and would not turn away from it. He worried it would fly away and he would miss seeing it go. He wondered what the hawk was hunting and in which direction it would fly. Its head turned, looking right at him. A perfect feeling of communion with nature mollified him, until he heard another sound inside his house, this time closer, louder, unmistakable. The hawk flew away.

He spun around to confront a frail-looking young woman standing in the doorway between his kitchen and the screened porch. She was just a girl. Caught in her long stringy hair, a tangled mess, her narrow, chapped hands wrung out an invisible rag.

"I'm sorry," she said, lip trembling. "I'm really, really sorry. I'm so sorry, Mister."

"What's happened?" he asked. "What do you want?"

She kept saying, "I'm sorry, I'm sorry, I'm so sorry, Mister."

He wondered what she was apologizing for, and why.

What was she sorry about?

Was she sorry for something she had already done to him, or for something she was about to do?

He had never seen her before, didn't even know who she was, or if she were alone.

She was trespassing.

He wondered if he were being robbed, perhaps by her accomplices.

He wondered if someone else was with her, somewhere else in his house, and if they were prepared to murder him.

Maybe it was all some sort of prank?

Perhaps a simple misunderstanding?

But she kept saying she was sorry?

Had she made some terrible mess, some terrible mistake?

Was she sorry for disturbing him, for showing up where she wasn't invited?

"I knocked," she said. "I knocked and I knocked. No one came.

Why didn't you come? I kept knocking and knocking. I knocked on the door, Mister. I did!"

"I believe you," said Geb.

"Then, I rang the bell. I tried, Mister. I kept pushing the button and pushing it, but I couldn't hear the bell."

The doorbell was broken, had been for years.

"I kept pushing the button. No one came. So, I started knocking, again," she said, now in tears.

Geb studied the girl closer — really examined her. She was wearing a long white short-sleeved cotton shirt patterned with abstract red flowers, petals painted in splotches. The flowers on her shirt seemed to be moving, blooming. The petals were blood drying.

"You're bleeding," he said, trying to remain calm.

"I was in an accident, down the road," she said. "We need help."

"Did you call the police? 9-1-1? What do you want me to do?" Geb asked. He had no way to call. His landline cut off; his cellphone stolen.

"No," she said. "My phone is in the car, with my friends."

"Come on," Geb said. "There's no phone here. I'll drive us."

"No," she said. "I'm not getting into another car." She turned, stumbling against the wall and upsetting coffee mugs on a shelf.

"Okay. Can we walk?" Geb asked.

The mugs shattered on the tile near her bloody tennis shoes.

Grabbing her elbow, Geb said, "Lead the way."

Geb planned to follow her to the accident, to see if anyone needed immediate assistance and then to run to the nearest convenience store to call for help.

She led him to the intersection where the tractor trailer accident had happened decades ago. It was a treacherous stretch of road, where an intersection met the bottom of a steep wooded hill. Chester Street dead-ended suddenly before the woods slid into a deep valley of vine-covered trees.

When they reached the intersection, he was surprised to find no wreck, no evidence of any accident.

"What's this?" Geb asked. "Where are your friends?"

"Down there," she said, pointing to the woods covered in vine.

He didn't see any vehicles or wreckage, only woods. He didn't know whether to believe her or not, but something in her eyes convinced him. Leaping off the asphalt, he began the steep trek down the hill, overgrown yet rocky. Earth slid beneath his shoes. He kept falling into the valley of chiggers and snakes. Losing his footing, he leapt into the drop-off. He tumbled. The ground gave way to a deep creek, hidden by a valley of cypress. He thrashed vines. The descent so sharp and rocky, he could only walk part of the way. Pebbles, mossy, slid underneath him, so he crawled and clawed down the hill before he started rolling, tumbling with rocks, gliding in mud.

At the very bottom, the creek covered in vine, it seemed as if it were dusk. He heard moaning and followed the moaning to an overturned Chevy Cruze beneath a broken tree. Beside the Chevy, an old Ford pickup tottered with a heavy-set man struggling, his battered arm dangling out the window. Near the pickup, a third vehicle, camouflaged in dirt and leaves and vines, rested at the lowest point in the creek.

The Chevy listed, a young man with a face masked in blood attempting to kick out the windshield from where he struggled against the crumpled dashboard inside the front seat. Trapped by a dented door, caged in fallen branches, two women inside the Chevy's backseat clawed at twigs, their manicured hands grasping. Their silver chain bracelets caught on splintered branches. Their brightly painted fingernails clashed against oak leaves.

Running to them, Geb hoisted the broken branches off the Chevy and dragged the women out of the open window of the passenger-side door. They shivered on the ground while gesturing to the young man with the blood-covered face. One woman clutched her left ankle. The other woman, crawling through the mud, kept slipping. Geb was afraid she would injure herself, but he realized he could not carry her up the steep incline slick with mud.

Smoke poured from the Chevy's hood. The two women screamed for the young man whose face was covered in blood. Bashing the glass with a grapefruit-sized rock, Geb shattered the Chevy's cracked windshield, and the young man tumbled out, his body limp. Caught in the branches, he dangled. Geb lifted him, carried him to the women, and laid him at their high heels. The woman with the injured ankle removed her blouse to wipe the blood away from the young man's eyelids.

Reaching into the Ford's open window, Geb turned off the engine and then took the pulse of the man inside the pickup. The man was barely conscious now, his crumpled legs crushed under the engine in his lap. Geb attempted to pry open the pickup's doors but couldn't.

"I'll get help," Geb said to the man, who remained unresponsive, though breathing.

Geb was about to rush up the hill when he remembered the third vehicle, the one so difficult to see. He approached the camouflaged vehicle, buried in dirt and leaves. He wiped them off, scooping both away with his hands. Karen and her mother sat inside the front seat. Mostly bone, they wore seatbelts. In the back seat, torn bags once holding groceries contained shredded plastic packages and discolored cans chewed by animals.

Geb started the long, slow, steep, and rough crawl back up the hill. On the road, covered in mud, he hitched to the convenience store, where the owner called the cops, accusing him of being a homeless man living in the woods. Geb begged the cops to venture down the hill to see what he had seen. Thankfully, the girl who had asked for his help was waiting on the road.

The paramedics arrived and freed the man from the pickup before loading all the victims onto stretchers to carry them up the hill.

After the ambulances drove away, Geb waited alone, near the dip of the hill. Since it was Sunday, the coroner took a long time to arrive. While waiting, Geb crawled back down the hill to the corpses in the darkening hollow. The darkness helped, as it was harder to see what had become of their faces.

# The Forgotten Daughter

Ansel and I used to date before he went to prison for killing my mother. He lived here in this apartment for months with her body and pretended she was still alive, so no one would kick him out. He strangled her and then beat her to death with a broomstick because he didn't want to be homeless. Then, he feared he would become homeless because he killed her. Now, he has free room and board in prison, for the rest of his life. Every time I pay my taxes, I'm paying his rent.

This bothers me almost as much as the closets I don't want to open and all the French doors, antique doors that are so hard to lock. And the upstairs bathroom with beautiful, gray-veined marble. It was Mother's favorite room, where Ansel wrapped her in trash bags and put her in the big marble bathtub, locked the door from the inside, leaving it closed, pretending nothing was wrong.

Every time I called or came over, he got rid of me fast. It was easy because Mother and I had a falling out, over him, so I thought she didn't want to talk to me, but I became nervous and felt guilty after not hearing from her for so many months.

"She's in the bathroom," Ansel said, "in the tub, and can't be disturbed."

Ansel's lies were true. He was a truthful person, perhaps too truthful.

For instance, he never bothered to hide his feelings about the apartment. The first time I brought him here to introduce him to Mother, he said, "I would kill for a place like this." I never took it literally. Even then, I was slow to realize.

✝ ✝ ✝

As a roommate, my mother kept me in the shadows by telling men she dated I was her sister. I didn't blame her. Our timing was off because she was very young when she gave birth to me. We were too close in age, when having a child was a death sentence to a young socialite. She never let me live it down, the carefree life I stole from her, all those parties, the way I depreciated her body, her status. She was less of a catch because whomever married her would have to take care of me. We were a package deal, where I lived as her conspirator and confidant, all along knowing I was the daughter she didn't want to have, especially in New York.

In my late teenage years, I went from being her conspirator to her rival, though I was slow to realize, never wanting to live that way. The men moved from one door to the other, in the night, in the dark. I pretended it was alright. She did the same. Both of our hearts were breaking for the opposite reason.

The three bedrooms of Mother's apartment with French doors open onto a terrace overlooking the building's courtyard garden. I remember gazing out the French doors as men entered my room, knowing when they pulled the curtains. Today, I got rid of all the curtains and feel safer when exposed.

With all these doors to lock, to check, to remember, I fear I've forgotten the feeling of Ansel's lips on my neck, giving me chills as he exhaled on my skin, whispering my name, long before I realized Mother had fallen in love with him or how much he had fallen in love with her apartment. He kept saying it was the perfect location, that he had always wanted to live in Tribeca. How could he afford it? He couldn't, but that didn't stop him from asking me when I would inherit and asking about Mother, visiting her often. At first, I was grateful. She was old and fragile by then, so I never imagined he was courting her. That he was kind to her was what seemed to matter most, the tenderness, as if it were his only inclination.

✣ ✣ ✣

Ansel's accommodations in prison must be a relief because he doesn't have to worry about the upstairs bathroom or the way I feel when I wake to hear French doors opening at night, when I'm sleeping in Mother's bed.

I moved back in more than a year after inheriting this place, when investigators and cleaners had done their work. The lawyer said to change the locks. I haven't yet because the building has security and the courtyard is gated, for residents only. Mother never gave the key to anyone other than Ansel and the cat sitter, and the cat died long ago.

I miss the cat.

I would say I miss Mother, but she was miserable in her last years, until Ansel came along and she was suddenly deliriously happy. That's why I'm not sure I really like the apartment anymore, now that it's mine. When I think of Mother and Ansel, I remember becoming homeless, when they looked at me and tried to explain why I would need to move out.

I understood what she had meant and why she took Ansel away, but now I have the apartment to myself and I'm all alone, wondering: does a single woman need three bedrooms and three bathrooms? No one bothers to ask me, just like no one bothered to ask my mother, though it was apparently on everyone's mind.

# Locked In

Nurses monitor my patient's vital signs. He has a rare reaction to drugs. Anesthesia makes him more alert and hyper-sensitive. It makes his heart race, instead of slowing it down. For him, depressives and sedatives provide no relief. Other than that, aside from being heavily tattooed, my patient, Dr. Rasch, is a healthy male in his mid-forties.

My assistant has given Dr. Rasch a paralytic, intubated and ventilated him.

He has to be "locked-in" and will remain conscious during surgery. Even knowing this, we both agreed to the procedure, though the hospital required mandatory meetings with a psychologist and bioethicist. After separate counseling sessions, Dr. Rasch and I had to sign legal waivers, in the presence of lawyers. We were always kept apart, not allowed to meet before the surgery.

The nurses must know what I'm going through. That's why none of the staff will look into my eyes. I don't blame them. I could barely stand to look into the mirror this morning because I've done what's needed. Tracing the complicated boundaries of his intricate tattoos on computerized simulation, I've marked where to cut, following a three-dimensional digital map of his skin.

I've drawn lines around the white monkey of his heart, the polar bears of his torso. I've traced the geometry of the lemurs on his left shoulder, the cobras behind his earlobes. The harpy owl of his belly glides near the golden eagle and gray wolves of his pelvis. The rhinos and jaguar storm a pride of lions lazing near the pelicans tattooed over his inner thighs. The snow leopards crouch near grizzly bears stalking great apes swinging on his arms.

His breathing is steady. He's doing well, though his eyes keep fluttering, following me. His hands flex, involuntarily, stroking the toucans and the pandas of his hips. None of this is supposed to happen under normal circumstances. But these are anything but normal.

In one intricate tattoo, the lioness lunges at the throat of a caribou on the side of my patient's hip. On the enlarged head of the lion, its tongue is covered in minuscule sharp hooks. In each hook, a tiny endangered bird soars.

I never wanted to be in this miserable position, where no choice is without suffering. If the press got word of what I'm taking from his tattoos, the public wouldn't understand how many animals have to suffer and die. Most people think every living thing is replaceable due to cloning, but they don't understand the underclass of female animals used to create clones. More importantly, they don't know about the bioterrorists who have destroyed bio-banks of animal DNA to prevent new additions to the underclass of female animals.

I feel guilty about the suffering of surrogate mothers. Whenever the DNA of an endangered species is used, most cloned fetuses die *in utero,* jeopardizing the health of surrogate mothers. Even when mothers from the same species can be found, hundreds of females are sacrificed, implanted with cloned embryos so big they cause agonizing births requiring Caesarean sections. Once an animal becomes a surrogate, she is bred to death. Most of her offspring die inside her or shortly after they are born.

Nevertheless, I slice just above my patient's femur, and blood gushes over this tattoo I'm excising, where a shrike lands on a cheetah's back under Dr. Rasch's right knee. Up Dr. Rasch's right leg, a baby raccoon swings from its mother's mouth, carried by the nape. Walking upright along his pubis, a soaked mother beaver carries her baby in her arms. A brood of opossums peek out of their mother's pouch near his groin.

After three hours of surgery, I am required to take a break. The operating room needs to be refreshed. On my way to change my scrubs, I see the television in the nurses' station. The last zoo animals, no longer able to breed, are paraded in front of cameras before calls for a massive culling. The government has already decided to start over again with new cloned animals created from the bio-bank.

The last captive animals fade into a shadow of their wild ancestors. Most people stopped visiting zoos years before they were outlawed. The zoos slowly shut down, and many of the last animals in captivity were taken on safari to be hunted by rich men seeking trophies. Mostly males have been shot, since they make better trophies. The females, those who have escaped the culling, will be forced into surrogacy.

When I return to the operating room, the nurses have turned my patient onto his side. The Nile crocodile of the enormous tattoo edges my patient's neck, where it holds its prey, twisting off a deer's limbs by spinning. The gill slits of the great white shark are full of falcons behind his right thigh near the golden eagle's huge talons.

I imagine animals fading in closed exhibits.

The smaller, more inbred a population, the more susceptible it is to a single harmful genetic mutation. Perhaps clones will increase the genetic diversity of the endangered population. That's why Dr. Rasch became a poacher, so researchers could access DNA from many different individual species being hunted to extinction.

He infiltrated their inner circle. He scavenged and froze blood, sperm, and umbilical-cord cells from the animals he hunted and saved the DNA in a safe place — the ink of his tattoos.

With every animal he killed, he added another tattoo to his body. Each tattoo housed DNA stored in microscopic capsules of a heat-controlled medical-grade Plexiglas. Sterilized and set in imperceptible acrylic beads of a synthetic resin, the DNA was enclosed, protected, and permanent. It would not degrade and could be surgically removed. Mixed into the ink, these beads were safe for injection since the non-biodegradable polymer never absorbed into his skin. The process was safe, or should have been, in theory, since the animal DNA wasn't actually injected into the skin but into the ink of his tattoos. Instead of disappearing into his body, the DNA floated, contained in ink. In hundreds of tattoos, thousands of animals' DNA was held tightly. Now, most of his skin must be removed to harvest that DNA.

I slice into his right calf, where young minks trail their mother as she hunts. Baby porcupines swing over branches. An African potto clings to a tree below three baby kangaroos resting on a spoon. Inside the rough scales of a beaver's tail, a stampede of wild horses emerges from dust. My scalpel gleams, glinting brightly as I think of all my patient and I have in common. We might have been friends, under different circumstances. I might have dated him, if I didn't have to skin him alive.

The hyena on his left shoulder blade stares at me with savage amber eyes. The sloth under his arm has a mischievous expression, as does the giraffe on the side of his left calf. Around his genitals, a giant squid and anaconda entangle with an octopus beside a great white shark, marlin, and sealions. All over his body, the cells of endangered animals thrive, hidden in plain sight, his tattoos mapping where to cut.

The nurses turn him over onto his belly before exposing his back and legs. The red fox and the bat-eared fox leap over his buttocks near the carrion crows of his lower spine. A barn owl captures a rattle snake on the back of his right femur. A horseshoe bat slides, the thin fabric of its wings spread across Dr. Rasch's back. Staring into the meshwork of wings, I see a camouflaged grid of sea anemones, starfish, seahorses, woodpeckers, and electric eels. Ready to begin excising the rest of the skin of his back, I cut and peel around his spine.

Now, I slice through the flesh of his ankle, carving, and he starts whimpering, talking, whispering. The nurses pause, frozen in horror.

"Is that him? He isn't supposed to be talking," a nurse says.

"Don't waste time," I say, realizing they think me callous, but every second we pause to express concern is a second longer he has to suffer.

No one is waiting for him in the waiting room. He's single, childless, and has already said goodbye to friends and family, who apparently think he's enjoying another long vacation, traveling the world.

On his travels, Dr. Rasch often befriended wealthy men who hunted lions and other magnificent creatures for sport. Whenever one animal was taken down, he collected samples of its DNA because he realized the DNA of animals captive for generations had deteriorated and needed to be refreshed by samples from the wild.

He shot lions.

He shot zebras.

He shot great apes.

He shot leopards.

He used a bow and arrow to take down eagles from the sky before returning to drink cognac in his glass-walled penthouse overlooking the biomedical facility where he worked, taking his hunting vacations on their dime. Trusting no one, not even his colleagues, he secretly began backing up the samples with his own private collection of animal DNA, stored where no one would think to look, in plain sight, within his tattoos, where the walrus pup hitches a ride on its mother's back. A sealion and a seal cruise blue water enveloping his thighs. The ivory tusk of a walrus gleams as it digs out shellfish on the bottom of the sea.

I remember the articles I read about Dr. Rasch in hunting magazines.

He slaughtered American buffalo.

He bled a blue whale and a school of dolphin.

An eccentric hunter, near his taxidermies, he posed nude to show his heavily tattooed body, only his hands, feet, and face untouched.

On his inner left shin, an aardvark with large ears and elongated snout appears almost tubular, its long tongue flicking out to Dr. Rasch's shinbone. Meanwhile, the duckbilled platypus dives, flexing its poisonous spur, as if underwater, its tiny eyes covered in fur, claws burrowing into the banks of rivers. Documenting his tattoos as body art, he made sure no one knew his plan, until it was necessary. I'm one of the few who will ever know because he's helpless on my table. He specifically asked for me to do this.

The nurses refresh my tray of instruments, again. New scalpels, scissors, saws, and tweezers gleam. As my patient's blood flows, my assistants suction near towels to stop the flood. Retractor, needle holder, forceps, towel clamps, hemostats — nothing is as helpful as my scalpel's fine edge, sharp enough to allow maximum control.

Typically, I save lives through skin transplants. Typically, when I take someone apart, I put him back together. I've worked with skin grafting on burn patients, accident victims, and victims of violence, trauma, infection, and skin cancer.

My movements are fluid and smooth. I could skin a man faster than any hunter could skin an animal, except that I must excise such complicated shapes, guided by the outline of Dr. Rasch's tattoos. I have turned his skin into a jigsaw puzzle. After excision, each puzzle piece is taken away on a tray, expertly packaged by medical technicians working for the bio-bank. Even with all the pieces to cut and tweeze, I work fast. I make no mistakes. Over the years, I have practiced on drumsticks, oranges, grapes, and chicken feet. I've mastered flap design and classification, the geometry of flaps, all the ways of planning surgical excisions.

Until now, I've done everything for my patients to prevent suffering, to avoid scars and tissue damage, to allow healing. Even if it meant animals sometimes had to die in various studies or in my surgical training.

So many animals have died to save human lives. The first serious attempts at xenotransplantation began in the early 1900s, when slices of rabbit kidney were transplanted into a child with renal failure. Since then, countless apes and pigs have died to provide organ transplants. Millions of mice have grown human tumors on their bodies. It's about time, as Dr. Rasch said in the video of his final will and testament (evidence recorded to keep me out of prison, or at least reduce my sentence), for humans to start dying to save the lives of animals.

A true innovator, Dr. Rasch experimented on his own body.

On his right hip, a brown bear stomps the salmons' spawning grounds. A massive clawed forepaw sweeps Dr. Rasch's right underarm to pin a salmon to the shallows. Meanwhile, a little spider monkey swings through the tree branches of my patient's rib cage, long legs and curved tail entwined with the leaves where doves hide. A troop of baboons with long bloody canines hunt, guided by two old males, in formation over Dr. Rasch's belly, toward his right hand, twitching.

Like Dr. Rasch, I want the zoo animals to live again. That's how I got involved. As a surgeon, I've never lost a patient before, and now I'm losing one on purpose. To make matters more complicated, my patient is a doctor, internationally celebrated for his body art, big game hunting, and research in genetics.

"My body, my life," he said in the videotaped will, "is a gift to the animals. I could feed myself to dying lions, or I could grow new ones."

The sea otter, swimming on its back, clutches a fish on its reddish-brown belly. The humpback whale's skin nodules are alive with barnacles full of many species of whale as I excise the pink flamingo in the cheetah's mouth.

I've watched Dr. Rasch's video many times, enough to be a believer. I have to be, since every excision will be full thickness, taking the epidermis and the entire thickness of the dermis. Here, in the snow den inside the hollow of Dr. Rasch's back, a mother polar bear suckles her cubs.

Despite what I know, I keep wondering if an intentionally fatal procedure makes a doctor a murderer. What if the patient isn't a victim but a willing life donor?

A chinchilla eats nuts near a wallaby where the fruit bat crawls over Dr. Rasch's hipbones. Here, a frightened hedgehog unrolls as a badger creeps over grass, unaware of the fortress hidden below, the burrow where the mother mole has birthed four pink babies in a cushioned nest lined with grass the color of the bush baby's enormous eyes.

I was warned not to speak to Dr. Rasch, mostly to protect myself. According to what the hospital administrators told me, he insisted on the procedure happening on the soonest date possible, due to cellular rejection he feared had already begun. "I'm losing them," he had said in the video. "I can't hold them much longer." He was particularly concerned with the giraffes of his elbows, or so I've been told. The monkeys are close to his heart, yet he worried they were leaving.

I excise the scorpion clutching a grasshopper in its pinchers near an Egyptian vulture, bald at the front of its face, cracking the bones of carrion by dropping them onto rocks. The chimpanzees, after killing and eating a baby baboon, are cleaning themselves with leaves, as I cut the black ink of their fur in sharp contrast to the red ink of blood.

Bioterrorists and animal rights activists never counted on a researcher like Dr. Rasch. A generous man, he's a prime example of informed consent, having known all the risks before he began his experiments. Though animal-to-human infection is rare, xenozoonosis is my fear. I've been warned about the dangers of cross-contamination with endogenous retroviruses, remnants of ancient viral infections, found in the genomes of mammals. They usually are not infectious in the host, but the virus may infect another species.

A weasel emerges from a tattooed tree hole, Dr. Rasch's navel. A prairie dog digs furiously in the dirt, where a mongoose cracks a cobra's skull.

I can't help but stare at what's left of his skin — still so many tattoos to cut away. On the exam table, Dr. Rasch is a seek-and-find of animals in cages. All the animals tattooed on his body I read about in childhood — big cats, great apes, bears, crocodiles, and raptors. I always wanted to go to a zoo, but zoos were already on their way to being outlawed, condemned, before I was a teenager. When I was a kid, my parents strongly objected, on moral grounds, calling the zoo an animal jail.

Dr. Rasch's eyes remain open as my assistants turn him, again. He sees. I know he sees. Through hundreds of incisions and excisions, he sees and feels and knows what's happening. He just isn't able to move voluntarily. No matter what happens, I've been told not to look into his eyes.

I try to heed this warning.

Though I was chosen for my training and experience in xenotransplantation, this is no xenograft. I complained only a little when required to speak to a board-certified psychologist approved by the surgical facility. Now, I take a deep breath and remember what the psychologist told me: I have to keep trying to understand Dr. Rasch's sacrifice. I have to find a way to appreciate it and make sense of it, or else I will be at risk due to the trauma of my work.

I know what happens to the skin I'm removing. A lab has to

remove the microscopic envelopes, the DNA captured in the ink of his animal tattoos. There is so much captured DNA of so many species that the excised skin has to be separated and shipped to different labs. The procedure has never been attempted before on this scale and requires over twelve hours of precise incisions. With at least two more hours remaining, I don't know if I can make it. In all my years of medical training, nothing has prepared me for such extensive excising.

I slice into him. Again, then again.

He bleeds and twitches and whispers words I can't understand.

I try not to listen to what he's whispering.

I try not to look into his eyes.

I keep cutting.

I peel his skin away, piece by piece, denuding his body, exposing veins, arteries, bones, and organs. The nurses have to keep holding his exposed organs with their gloved hands to keep them from falling to the floor.

Wiping more blood away, the nurses make sure the remaining tattoos are visible as I cut.

I slice the armadillo's suit of bony armor camouflaged in the shadow of two bighorn rams smashing horns over an ewe. Beneath Dr. Rasch's thorax, hippos clash, lip to lip, in wide open-mouth courtship. I take strips of remaining skin off his abdomen and groin. I peel a patch of skin above the clavicle. I strip even more skin from his legs, hips, back, and chest. With each cut, I'm targeting the next priority, according to the detailed instructions provided by the hospital. As agreed, I excise my patient's tattoos in a prescribed order, according to digital maps made of his skin.

I try to think of the lives we are saving, not the life I am taking. This exquisite man, genius and gorgeous. Despite my admiration for him, I mutilate him slowly, precisely. I move onto the next tattoo on the excision list. Turned onto its back, a hedgehog rolls in a defensive ball near a porcupine, quills erect. A two-toed sloth sleeps in clouds of mist. As I begin to slice away at his right inner wrist, Dr. Rasch twitches, almost imperceptibly. I wonder if it's my imagination. Our eyes meet. In those eyes, I see forgiveness. At least I hope I do.

I was twelve years old when the last captive giraffe fell in Europe, culled in public for educational purposes. I was sixteen when the last wild zebra walked the earth. The last wild elephant gone before I could speak, these mystical creatures haunted my dreams. Apparently, Dr. Rasch loved zoo animals as much as I did — or as much as I thought I did before the culling. Now there are no more open zoos or tigers or lions or bears on display, only a few hidden in closed facilities before being culled, released to be hunted on safari, or held as surrogates. Many of the last zoo animals were culled after the zoo closings, death considered more humane than captivity.

On Dr. Rasch's left leg, I excise a jaguar. On his right bicep, I take a snow leopard. Over the remaining skin of his chest, I carve out a harpy eagle, and inside the feathers of the giant eagle are other eagles, raptors so tiny they nestle inside the down. An elephant on his neck is filled with hidden crocodiles, visible only under a medical magnifying glass. The peacock on his thigh houses lizards. A hippo bathes above his right elbow near the cobra and the silver back chasing flamingos.

I only want the animals to live, again, so I can see them with my own eyes.

The brown pelican dives through the air to catch its prey on the edge of Dr. Rasch's left ankle near a piranha with razor-sharp triangular teeth. Inside each scale of the piranha are tiny zebras, Indian tigers, hatchet fish, carpet sharks, geckos, leopards, praying mantises, and snowy owls hunting prey so small they can only be seen under the lens of a surgical microscope.

Dr. Rasch is Noah's Ark. He put a bit of every animal into his tattoos, to save them from leaving the earth. Now I want to save him, so I steal a vial of his blood — and keep it as my own. The nurses pause but say nothing. I want to have Dr. Rasch's DNA tattooed on me and to find a way to bring him back. I remember we can only clone the body, never the soul.

His body now resembles wet red patchwork, so many pieces of skin cut away that only thin shreds remain to link patches.

For now, I do what the psychologist asked. I remind myself: in my childhood, people started to feel the vast emptiness of a world without wild animals. I was the first generation to experience how the missing animals became the obsession of children. Lions, giraffes, alligators, zebras, and bears were the new dinosaurs. There were so many movies about bringing them back to life.

I never saw a zoo, outside of photographs and television and descriptions in history books. By the time I was born, many of the species once held by zoos were extinct. They no longer existed in the wild, their habitat gone. No more gorillas, lions, tigers, bears. No more giraffes, hippos, or elephants. No more harpy eagles or pandas.

Perhaps my patient's intricate ink hides a new type of cage, trapping animals in a high-tech way. A flying squirrel glides into the den of Dr. Rasch's left underarm hollow. The nocturnal solenodon sticks its head into a hole near a bison beside Dr. Rasch's armpit.

Still skinning him alive, even though I know he's going to change the world, I forgive a sudden selfish thought: how I might have loved him! I could have read his tattoos like a novel in bed every night before turning out the lights. As the sun washed over his naked body in the morning, he could have whispered to me without speaking. His ink tells stories, even now, as I strip and pull a narrow flap of skin with clamps and tweezers.

Slowly, I finish excising the last strips, the narrow flaps of his chest. It's like peeling an orange with a knife. Only the skin of his feet, his hands, and his face remains. The nurses remove the ventilator, yet somehow, Dr. Rasch still breathes. His heart still beats. He inhales and exhales, slowly but steady. He should be gone now. I know. We all know. He should be leaving. He could have left us minutes, or even hours, ago.

The nurses look at me, as if wondering what to do. This wasn't supposed to happen. I see it in their eyes, but I don't tell them what we already know because I'm afraid he might hear me. It's too terrible to put into words. We are finished with him, but he's not gone. He should be leaving, but his heart is still beating.

# Acknowledgements

Grateful acknowledgment is made to journals and other publications in which some of these works have appeared:

*The Adroit Journal* ("The Forgotten Daughter")

*Arkansas Review: A Journal of Delta Studies* ("Abandoned Nest" as "Squirrel Patrol")

*Bellingham Review* ("Ducky")

*Best Short Stories from The Saturday Evening Post Great American Fiction Contest 2019.* The Saturday Evening Post Society ("The Ambassador Owl" as "Fishing for Owls")

*Big Other* ("What Goes on Near the Water")

*Dislocate* ("The Shadow Family" as "Lessons from a Sinaloa Beauty Queen")

*Lake Effect* ("The Open Invitation" and "Theatrum Insectorum")

*The Laurel Review* ("The Mushroom Suit")

*L'IRCOCERVO: LA RIVISTA "La Figlia Dimenticata."* ("The Forgotten Daughter")

*Litro NY* ("Locked In" as "The Last Zoo")

*Savoy Operetta* ("Joe and Irish")

Thank you to Patrick Davis for his insights and for encouraging me to search for the anti-story in the story. Thank you to everyone at Unbound Edition Press. Thank you to Rachele Salvini for her translation of "The Forgotten Daughter." Thank you to John Madera for edits on "What Goes on Near the Water." Thank you to Luke Rolfes for helpful comments on "Longtime Passing."

# About the Author

Aimee Parkison, recognized for her experimental fiction about women and her revisionist approach to narrative, has won numerous awards and fellowships. These include: a Christopher Isherwood Fellowship; the Catherine Doctorow Innovative Fiction Prize from Fiction Collective Two; the Kurt Vonnegut Prize from *North American Review;* the Starcherone Prize for Innovative Fiction; the Jack Dyer Prize from *Crab Orchard Review;* a North Carolina Arts Council Fellowship; a Writers at Work Fellowship; a prize for writing on madness from *Fiction International;* a Puffin Foundation Fellowship; a William Faulkner Literary Competition Award for the Novel; and an American Antiquarian Society Creative Artists Fellowship. Parkison is the author of *Refrigerated Music for a Gleaming Woman,* winner of the Fiction Collective Two Catherine Doctorow Innovative Fiction Prize, which was published in 2017 by FC2/University of Alabama Press. Her other works include *Woman with Dark Horses* (Starcherone, 2004), *The Innocent Party* (BOA Editions, Ltd., American Reader Series 2012), *The Petals of Your Eyes* (Starcherone/Dzanc, 2014), and *Sister Séance* (KERNPUNKT, 2021). Parkison has taught creative writing at a number of universities, including Cornell University, the University of North Carolina at Charlotte, and Oklahoma State University, where she is a Professor of Fiction Writing. Parkison has taught as a visiting faculty member at the British Council's International Creative Writing Summer School in Athens, Greece, and as a fiction faculty member at Chautauqua Writers' Festival.

aimeeparkison.com

# About the Type and Paper

Designed by Malou Verlomme of the Monotype Studio, Macklin is an elegant, high-contrast typeface. It has been designed purposely for more emotional appeal.

The concept for Macklin began with research on historical material from Britain and Europe dating to the beginning of the 19th century, specifically the work of Vincent Figgins. Verlomme pays respect to Figgins's work with Macklin, but pushes the family to a more contemporary place.

This book is printed on natural Rolland Enviro Book stock. The paper is 100 percent post-consumer sustainable fiber content and is FSC-certified.

*Suburban Death Project* was designed by Eleanor Safe and Joseph Floresca.

Unbound Edition Press champions honest, original voices.
Committed to the power of writers who explore and illuminate
the contemporary human condition, we publish collections of poetry,
short fiction, and essays. Our publisher and editorial team aim
to identify, develop, and defend authors who create thoughtfully
challenging work which may not find a home with mainstream
publishers. We are guided by a mission to respect and elevate
emerging, under-appreciated, and marginalized authors, with
a strong commitment to advancing LGBTQ+ and BIPOC voices.
We are honored to make meaningful contributions to the literary arts
by publishing their work.

unboundedition.com